THE SAVAGE JOY OF BATTLE

Holding the torch, Torr turned towards the door he had left open and now the sudden press of soldiery that filled it had no obstruction. Spears and swords flamed redly in the torchlight glare. The savage joy of battle coursed through Torr's whole being. He felt byoyed up, exalted, transfigured. He exulted in the strife. Yet he did not chant some barbaric war-song as the heathen might do . . . he had learned his fighting in a tougher school than the barbarian nomads could know.

SWORDS OF THE BARBARIANS

by

KENNETH BULMER

BELMONT TOWER BOOKS ● NEW YORK CITY

A BELMONT TOWER BOOK

Published by

Tower Publications, Inc.
185 Madison Avenue
New York, N.Y. 10016

Printed in the United States of America.

Contents

I

Torr and Tara in Gamelon Town

The moral of this imbroglio, Torr chuckled to himself as he ducked a wildly swung club and leaped a market stall keeper who clutched screeching for his legs, taught him that next time he was forced to seize a chicken he should better remember the hard lessons of his youth.

How Tara would mock him now!

The late evening market of Gamelon Town seethed with housewives and slaves and purveyors all clamouring to complete their business in the windy light of torches before the gathering storm struck. Banners cracked stiffly above the battlements of the time-worn walls. The exotic hues and spicy scents and shrill barterings blended into a background against which the figure of Torr Vorkun of Darkholm, if taller and wider than average, should yet have passed unnoticed.

Yet his first attempt at bargaining with a stallkeeper resulted in this dismaying if enjoyable hue and cry.

Everyone in Gamelon grew red hair on their ugly heads, that was the truth of it.

Apples and multi-hued fruits from strange foreign lands sprayed from overset stalls. Awnings split with raucous rippings as fat men staggered back from Torr's swinging arms. The bedlam raged.

'Thief! Outlander! Bring him down! Beat out his brains!'

'By the swag belly of Obese Rumphaldi Himself! I'm no thief!' roared Torr. He shoved a gesticulating man over into a pile of pots and cascaded an avalanche of pots and cups across the cobbles. 'I just don't happen to have any of your decadent money! Out of my way, riff-raff!'

He roared across the market leaving a swathe of devastation

in his wake. The chicken swung by its legs and squawked and fluttered its wings. Torr felt the familiar weight of his broadsword slung from his belt. He left it lie in its scabbard. This was no work for Lycheaper.

He ducked a flung cobblestone, butted a fat man where wind and water met, leaped a stall of stinking fish too long netted from the Opal Sea and raced, shouting with laughter, into the black net of alleys surrounding the market place. The rout hallooed at his heels.

No sorcery was likely to be hurled at him from the crowd. They kept their towers these days, did the sorcerers of Gamelon Town, quaking in their shoes trying to influence the coming invasion from Garthland and the inevitable war. A strange place, this, to Torr Vorkun, a young man not unacquainted with strange corners of his world, and yet one he might have grown to like had he the means to pay his way.

Several ways presented themselves and he chose the narrowest and darkest. Storm clouds gathered above the rooftops and the wind whistled with a keener bite on the evening air. He ran with the long loping stride of the superb athlete he was, and yet in his every movement the wariness and the alert expectancy of the born fighter displayed clearly how in an age of sudden death he had remained alive for five and twenty years.

So it was that the four guards who came on him around a crumbling corner of mouldering brick where a single torch sputtered from its iron bracket against the darkness ran not into a helpless man fleeing from a mob but a fiercely prepared warrior.

The guards' halberds lowered, their points glinting.

Torr Vorkun laughed again and ran in without halting.

The sergeant of the guard, him with the bronze helmet and the red sash of office, shouted – once.

'Take the foreign devil alive!'

Then he shouted no more as Vorkun forced up the halberd, wrenched it free and struck once – twice – thrice. The fourth guard stood for a single frozen instant, his mouth hanging open. Then with a screech of pure fright he dropped his weapon and turned and ran. His fierce eyes filled with savage glee, Torr hurled the halberd after the guard. He roared with laughter as the shaft tangled the man's legs, brought him down in a tumble of rolling helmet and tangled accoutrements.

'When the Garthlanders get here you'd best fight better than that, fellow! By the stinking armpit of Obese Rumphaldi Himself! They'll chop you finer than best mince!'

Then he looked around with a curse. The chicken had vanished. Squawking, it had leaped free. Now, Torr Vorkun of Darkholm of Drugay was supperless once more.

The rout bayed in the next alley.

He shouted an insult at the petrified guard and took himself off, not well pleased.

Since Tara and he had arrived in Gamelon Town after tramping across the great plains and traversing the dismal defiles of the Forest of Stretting they had found themselves squalid lodgings, eaten one stingy meal on the proceeds of the last of Tara's bangles and were still no nearer finding the wizard Jaran the All-Seeing. His attempts at bargaining for a chicken had ended in insults and a hot-headed snatch. Food these days under the stress of forthcoming war had increased in price and decreased in supply.

'By Gitanji the Gourmet!' he rumbled. 'Better for us to shake the filthy dust of Gamelon Town from our boots!'

He moved on along squalid alleys, beneath overhanging balconies close-shuttered, into vagrant pools of light from scattered torches and plunging into the soft shadows between. Accustomed to the wild free life of the open plains and the sheer-walled mountains of his youth towns gave him a fretting sense of confinement, even after his long sojourn in Paltomir, the greatest city of the League of Praterxes.

His straight soft-brown hair hung almost to his shoulders, confined by a single strap of good curlish leather without embroidery of other finery. His tunic and breech-clout, too, had been crudely fashioned by a hunch-backed dwarf in far off Khurdisrane from softened curlish leather. But his belt from which hung the scabbard of his true sword Lycheaper and his knee-high riding boots had been well-made in Paltomir the Blessed itself, from the tough hide of the wild and ferocious dragobrane. The hunt in which he'd started and finally killed that dragobrane had been roundly sung and storied by all the bards of Paltomir, not least by old Grendan, the Lord Hight King's harper of golden melody. Yes, they had been good times, when he'd been a captain in the guard of the Lord High King. But at the first whisper that the sorcerer Jaran the All-Seeing might possess the answers to the questions Torr and Tara of Darkholm and Drugay had quested since first they could talk he had left Blessed Paltomir and set his face towards the plains and forests.

And now, here he was, skulking through stinking back alleys, supperless.

How, by the profane name of Chomath the Defiled, could he face his twin sister Tara empty-handed?

As though the tenuous and inexplicable link that bound them at times of peril had been sharpened by his own shamed thoughts of her, Tara's voice shocked into his mind.

'Torr! I am beset! Beasts in the guise of men! Torr – Help!'

Without thought, without pause Torr Vorkun of Dragay raced wide-mouthed and gulping foetid air through the sullen tangle of alleys. He did not pause for a single heartbeat to question, to doubt, the reality of that thin ghostly voice that whispered in his brain. Only when in dire danger could that uncanny link between twin and twin function. Now, of a certainty, Tara faced peril that, being only guessable, was all the more terrible for that.

The pursuit from the market place had been thrown off. He raged down the alleys, vaulting heaps of rotting refuse, hurdling open drains, until he came to the leaning wooden stair leading up to the single room they had bargained a bangle for. A few torches scattered light that emphasised the shadows. Stained walls and shuttered windows crowded close. He could hear the noise as he put his foot on the first worm-eaten tread.

Hoarse men's voices, raised in coarse laughter and ribald witticisms, pelted the night with profanity. A chill wind gusted. Somewhere a loose shutter clacked. He padded up the treads like a black beast from the night and as he went he drew Lycheaper from the scabbard.

Again Tara's ghostly voice echoed in his mind. No panic, no screaming blind terror that would oust reason, rode in with that whispering voice in his head. Yet there must be deadly peril for Tara to call so vehemently.

A resonant voice boomed beyond the closed and rickety door.

'Treat the girl gently. We want her for our pleasuring! Not for blood sport!'

A sound of a soggy blow and a man's abrupt 'Oof!'

A roar of laughter, then : 'By Tremineds, the girl fights well for her honour!'

Feet scuffling on the floor, the crash of their single chair overturning, hoarse panting, lascivious laughter – all brought Vorkun up the stairs with his naked brand in his fist.

He kicked the door open.

By the light of a torch thrust into a becket by the door – a light brought by the would-be rapists – he saw five men grappling with Tara and a sixth sitting doubled-up on the floor clutching his belly and groaning. They were all clad in the loose puce tunics and white cloaks of the Gamelon soldiery, much bedizened with embroidery, their helmets laid aside, their swords still clasped in scabbards. Fierce merciless faces stared wolfishly on Tara as she struggled with them.

'Foreign witch! She devil!' they were yelling as they pawed and groped and tried to hold her down.

'You gutter-bred impotent slug-worms!' she blazed, razoring fingernails down a bearded cheek. 'You limp-weaponed filth-eating znunderbug offal!'

The struggle reeled across the floor. The table crashed over. Another man staggered away holding his guts, gurgling with pain, vomiting.

'By all the devils in Sintian! She fights like a she-wolf!'

'Witch! Throw yourself on our mercy!'

A roaring string of epithets ripped from Tara that made Torr almost smile with pride. Apart from her knee-high riding boots, twins to those worn by Torr, Tara of Darkholm of Drugay struggled stark naked.

But no laughter could touch Torr Vorkun of Drugay now. No light-hearted romp of combat, no joyous blood-singing battle – not when his sister was being mauled by men like this.

Magnificent she was, gorgeous in all the pride and womanliness of youth and health and beauty. Tanned and smooth, her

11

skin glowed. Her hair, of the same soft-brown colour as her brothers, hung a little longer, a little silkier. Pride and love clutched at Torr Vorkun as he gazed on his twin sister, acknowledged the fairest of all women in the world.

Her figure maddened the soldiers of Gamelon Town. They pressed in, grasping and groping, trying to capture her pummelling arms and kicking legs. Yet they saw with amazement that continually she sought to strip from herself those soft-leather riding boots, sought to strip herself completely naked.

'Hold the witch down!' and 'My prize! She has wounded me for life!' and 'Crack her over the head, Karl, and have done!'

Torr took a single step into the room.

His broadsword lifted, the light running down the blade in crooked whirlicues of brilliance.

He did not bother to shout a warning, a challenge, a defiance. He simply rushed straight in. The pommel of Lycheaper smashed down on to red-haired head, driving a man on to his face on the floor. Torr's left hand ripped a sweating neck up out of the ruck, hurled its owner bone-breakingly against the wall. The flat of the blade crushed a nose and cheekbone into a red jelly.

Then the others whipped their swords out, slim curved scimitars with jewelled hilts.

Now Vorkun of Darkholm spoke.

'So you wish to make this fight for real? Well – any man who lays a hand on my sister dies! So, dogs – die!'

They hurled themselves on him. They were three to one.

The naked form of Tara of Drugay spun from the fight. Yet, absorbed, she continued to tug and pull at her left boot, cursing horribly, trying to unbuckle the jammed straps.

'Cut the foreigner down! He is but one! On him!'

Three scimitars flashed towards Torr's breast.

He caught the first on the forte of Lycheaper, twisted, ducked a wild swing and kicked the third man in the groin. Then his blade slid smoothly forward, between the fourth and fifth ribs of the second man. The first man, long before his city-slowed reflexes could turn him, saw his death swing diagonally shoulder high to embed the crimsoned blade deep in the angle of neck and shoulder.

Torr Vurkun had not struck with full force; the soldier's head remained on his shoulders.

Now Torr leaped agilely sideways, from a striking position moving instantly to headlong movement. The man who had been doubled-up over his belly had risen and with a quick stealthy movement had tried to stab Torr in the back. As Torr cut him down, he yelled: 'Hey! Tara! Your fool boot! That scum might have –'

Tara looked up with hot eyes. 'If you can't handle six louts like this you're no true Drugayan! Once I get this Amadis-forsaken boot off, I'll –'

The enjoyment of battle he had scorned when his sister lay in peril returned now. Laughter bubbled up.

'Sure! And what happened to Kastrader?'

Tara flung a mean glance at her brother and nodded then towards a corner. On the wall by its belt hung her sword Kastrader, a blade after the fashion of Lycheaper but of necessarily lighter heft. She did not cease from her attempts to pull off her boot.

'They jumped me when I was brushing my hair –'

'Well, these four will jump no more.' He faced the man he had flung against the wall and whose face he had smashed, and the man whose skull he had crushed with Lycheaper's pommel. 'I think these two, likewise, will fill a vulture's belly.'

'So.' She looked up at her brother and some of the hotness melted from her eyes, so that they smiled their long glancing smile of love and sisterly affection. 'You were long enough getting here.'

'Leave your boot, Tara. They're all dead.' His grimness returned so that, for a moment, his strong young face with the straight nose and clear brown eyes took on the semblance of a devil staring from the smoky pits of hell. 'They asked for death, to dare lay a finger on you – Tara –'

'And there will be others coming and this damned boot buckle is jammed fast!'

As she worked with slim fingers over the jammed buckle, her long back bent into a curve of purest poetry and her firm maidenly breasts trembling, she presented a picture that etched

13

itself into Torr's mind so that somewhere within him an old ache awoke and clawed at him with mocking fingers he had thought long ago loosened and forgotten.

'You are right – sister,' he said harshly.

She looked up abruptly, frowning.

'Why – We agreed never to call each other brother or sister, rather brother and brother for many times has it been necessary for me to masquerade as your brother – '

'I know.' Torr spoke brutally. 'I said sister to remind myself that you are my twin sister.'

He bent and began to wipe Lycheaper on the white cloak of one of the dead men.

'But still you are right. There will be others. We must go at once. Start putting your clothes on instead of taking them off.'

She pouted at him, suddenly a mischevious slip of a girl. However, she left off tugging her boot buckle and began to don her tunic and breechclout. She knew when to argue with her twin and when to agree.

Taking up the torch Torr waited by the door. Apart from what they stood up in they had no other possessions. They had even lost their short swords, companions to Lycheaper and Kastrader. In the pouch at Tara's waist were a comb and brush, a hunk of lavastone, a pair of tweezers not of silver but of common metal and a few other trifles.

'I am ready,' she said.

Holding the torch, Torr turned towards the door. He had left it open when he had burst in and now the sudden press of soldiery that filled it had no obstruction. Spears and swords flamed redly in the torchlight glare. Venemous faces and startled eyes lit on the shambles within. A sharp imperious voice lifted.

'Take the foreign devils alive!'

Vorkun of Darkholm did not hesitate. The torch spat lividly as he flung it full in the faces of the front rank of soldiers. Lycheaper howled as he dragged it forth from the scabbard. With a wild yell he hurled himself after the torch.

There were a full two score of them and they rolled up the stairs faster than Torr could hurl them aside. The crimson

14

blade of Lycheaper reeked with the smoke of mortal combat. At his side Kastrader leaped and darted and tore into living human flesh, a sure guard and shield.

The savage joy of battle coursed through Torr's whole being. He felt buoyed up, exalted, transfigured. He exulted in the strife. Yet he did not chant some barbaric war-song as the heathen might do. He had learned his fighting in a tougher school than the barbarian nomads could know.

An arrow sliced through the open door and stuck quivering in the wall. A second stripped a long red sliver of skin from the bulging muscles of his arm. Vaguely he glimpsed archers in the press, bows bent, arrows nocked, the deadly points aimed for his heart.

'Tara!' he yelled in a cracking voice. 'The window! Run for it! Break through! I'll hold them off here!'

He did not feel the arrow that glanced from his temple except afterwards, as he lay on the floor with all his head engulfed in the red roaring haze of pain. He saw the soldiers drag Tara away, writhing, battling still, her tunic half-torn from her body. Her face thrust agonisedly back. She screamed after her brother.

'The mad foreign devil is dead!' snapped that high thin voice. Leave him for the carrion thongs. Take the girl. I shall enjoy taming her to more pleasant ways!'

And then darkness clutched Torr Vorkun of Darkholm in iron fetters beyond all pain.

2

The Peril of Cheap Boot Buckles

Thunder grumbled and grunted maliciously from the dark sky over Gamelon Town. The wind dashed the first drops of the coming downpour against closed windows and barred doors. The soldiers drew their white cloaks more closely around their puce tunics, the wind ruffling and tossing the plumes in their bronze helmets. Spear butts and iron-shod sandals rang on the cobbles.

In the wild light of a streaming torch Tara could see the officer with the high thin voice. His dark face with the beak nose and vulpine lips leered down on her. She tore her gaze away as a white rabbit seeks to avoid a snake, twisting and struggling to look back into the single room beyond the half-closed door.

Torr Vorkun lay where he had fallen. The arrow was clearly visible, its head buried in Torr's temple, the dark blood dropping down.

'My brother!' Tara shrieked. Like an untamed dryne who in his first day of breaking feels the saddle and the spur, she writhed and contorted. Her long legs flashed out to kick and her fists sought targets blindly in the flaring light. Rough hands caught and imprisoned her. Her eyes satiated themselves in a last long look on her brother. A bitter sob broke through her passionate hatred of these men and she felt a treacherous weakness chilling her guts. That all their high hopes should end like this!'

'Take her away and don't mark her!' snapped the officer. He carried the stamp of authority derived from the golden-trimmed sash that crossed his narrow chest. 'And take her sword – and that of the murdered! These barbarians are but cavalry-fodder; but oftimes they wield good blades.'

Obedient soldiers scooped up Kastrader and Lycheaper.

'I'm no barbarian, townie!' gasped Tara.

A stinging back-hand blow crushed her full lips.

'Silence, bawd. I shall teach you manners – later.'

Thereafter they marched in a clump through the noisome alleys of Gamelon Town which, despite its battlemented walls and three centuries' old castle keep, is yet a poor place of dirt and smell and narrowness to be the second capital of all the March of Gamelon itself. Out of the south east had Torr and Tara came, by way of battles and strife and brief sojourns in outlandish places where sorceries ruled, leaving far on the other side of the world their steading of Darkholm in the fair land of Drugay, serving most recently at the court and in the guard of the Lord High King of Paltomir the Blessed. Now it seemed to the girl as she was dragged, partly by her arms, partly by her silken brown hair, through the mud and filth of the alien cobblestones, that their search for Jaran the All-seeing had ended, finally, in utter hopelessness and defeat.

Of what use now his powers of searching all time past and all time to come when they could never reach him, when she was as prisoner, when Torr was – She struggled again then, ignoring the pain as the soldiers tugged her hair, refusing to think the words describing Torr let alone give tongue to them and thus in the shadowy way of necromancy give them power and weight.

'Come along, girl! It's no use struggling! By Tremineds, bawd, if you don't stop this I'll crack you over the head myself!'

The thin face glared into her own as the soldiers dragged back on her hair.

'May Amadis turn her face away from you, znunderbug-offal!'

The officer slapped her across the face, hard, his harsh features fixed and hating.

'Drag her!' he snapped. 'Her spirit will break to mine or my name is not Prando the Unsleeping.'

'Prando the Eversleeping,' she whispered through bloody lips, 'if I get my hand around Kastrader's hilt again!'

Past a line of swirling torches reflecting on the brazen helmets and curved blades of watchful sentries they marched into the keep of the castle of Gamelon Town. Hewn stone in unmortared tiers raked towards the cloud-tossed sky. Rain splattered and streaked the walls and set the torches sizzling. Iron-shod sandals clanged on stone and roused weird echoes. Shadows closed in.

Expecting to be flung into a foul and foetid cell Tara experienced a fresh chill as she was led up stone stairways and through draped tapestry curtains into a furnished apartment halfway up the north-east tower. Tapers burned uneasily, casting shifting light across stuffed cushions, tables with beast-clawed legs, chests with their lids flung back disclosing costly silks and cloths, a board laid with a white napkin on which glinted silver cutlery and white china from distant Tremiphond.

'Strap her to the bed!' commanded Prando the Unsleeping.

The soldiers bore Tara down, spreadeagled her, used belts to bind her wrists and ankles to the bed's four posts. Prando, when their work was finished, cursed them out of his chamber, and then turned to regard his prisoner.

He picked up a chased golden goblet and sniffed a delicate moment at the wine's aroma. Then he tossed back his head and drained the cup. He flung it into a corner.

Refusing to comment, Tara lay still.

If only those thrice-accursed buckles had not jammed!

She felt a hot wave of resentment. Of fear she would have no truck. Only one thing mattered to her now; to get away from this place and back to their lodgings to see what must be done with Torr – to nurse him, or to keen over his lifeless body.

Standing over her, Prando bent forward, reaching out to let her silky brown hair fall through his fingers.

'So smooth,' he said breathily. 'So fine – and brown!'

'Aye, brown,' she said. 'A sure mark of a foreigner in this cursed town of red-polls!'

Some deep well of evil good humour animated Prando the Unsleeping now. He took up the two swords and balanced them, Lycheaper in his right, Kastrader in his left. He studied the plain steel hilts with their open-work smooth with long use. His small hand fitted illy within the space that Torr Vorkun would fill with his own square right hand, leaving enough room for a double-handed grasp if the need arose; and even Kastrader made Prando's thin puniness look even sicklier.

'Good swords, as I guessed,' the Gamelon officer mused. 'Strange brands for avowed witches and warlocks.'

Tara cocked an eye at him.

'Witch?' she said.

He smiled, putting the swords by. 'You worked a magic on a small girl in your house of lodging –'

'But I took away a headache! A simple thing – '

'Aye! But you did this thing, simple or no, without medicaments, withouts herbs or potions. You passed your hands over her brow and intoned a spell, and –'

'And so that's why a high officer of the Gamelon army arrests me – that's my thanks for helping a small child!'

'Sorcery may be practiced here only by the accredited necromancers of Gamelon! You have twice sinned. Your life is forfeit!' He smiled down on her. 'Unless –'

She twisted her head from side to side. The thick brocade of the bed covering felt hard and edged against her cheeks. She looked straight up at Prando the Unsleeping.

'Unless?' She made her lips curve into a smile answering his own. 'I'm never at ease on a bed,' said Tara Vorkun of Darkholm, 'with all my clothes on.'

His breath caught thickly in his throat. His eyes widened. 'You – ?'

'My boots. They are hot and they pain me. The buckles are stuck. You'd best begin there –'

He laughed softly. 'I think, little witch, I will leave the boots until the last. For I have a picture in my mind of you – a picture I would see before I pleasure myself more grossly.'

With the razor point of Kastrader he flicked down on the latches of her tunic, already half-torn away. He flicked the curlish leather aside, daintily, baring her breasts. Finickily he cut away the knots of her breechclout. Fuming, Tara lay helplessly bound. Those thrice-cursed, Amadis-forsaken boot buckles. Would this slavering lout never loose them?

She rolled aside, her tanned flesh smooth and gleaming in the tapers'-light.

19

'My boots hurt me!' she said sharply. 'I cannot be all you would wish if I am suffering –

Something in what she said amused him; but he bent to the buckle of her left boot. His thin brown fingers began to pluck at first indifferently as he stared up along the length of her body, and then more irritably as the buckle refused to dislodge its tang. He ripped away at the buckle with a savage curse, making the leather cut into the tender flesh beneath her knee.

A quick rap on the door snapped him up with a ripped curse. A soldier marched in, saluting, his face blank.

'Corlon Prando – the watch – there is strange news – '

'By the stinking vomit of Black Nargoth! All right. I will be with you!'

The soldier saluted again and swung about. Smiling his small frozen smile, Prando the Unsleeping stepped away from the bound form of Tara.

'I will not be long. Wait for me, she witch. Do not run away from my hot embraces!'

Roaring his laughter at his own witticism, Prando the Unsleeping stalked out of the chamber. For a moment, Tara relaxed. Then she began to work at the belts binding her to the bed-posts. She was still working away and making not the slightest impression when, some time later, Prando returned. He looked in an ill-humour; but at sight of the girl his lascivious good humour returned. He bent across to caress her naked body.

'My sweet little witch-girl!'

'My boots!'

He chuckled, deep in his throat.

'Very well – your boots. And then, maiden, and then!'

3

The Thing in the Smoke

The pain lurched back as a dull ache down the side of his head, rimmed in red and swathed in darkness. He opened his eyes to see the grimed boards of the floor. He had suffered pain before and knew how to live with it. He sat up and felt his head gingerly. The arrow still stood there, wet with blood. He felt the curlish leather hair strap, and the arrowhead lodged between it and his scalp as though punched clean into his very brain, and he understood how he had escaped.

With a savage curse Torr Vorkun ripped the arrow out and flung it from him. The greatest bowman of Drugay itself, he knew when the gods of fortune smile on a man.

'May Szangkill the Archer, whose shaft never misses, be praised!'

He dabbed at his head, feeling the gash and knowing the wound, like the scratch along his arm, would not halt him. Quickly he established what had happened here, and seeking Tara and Lycheaper and Kastrader and not finding them, he turned his bloody face towards the Gamelon night.

'The Keep! By Chomath the Defiled! That's where Tara is -- and the swords, too.'

Without any further thought he padded down the steps, avoiding the spilt blood, noticing that the corpses of those he had slain had been removed. Soon the scavengers would report that his body had gone. What they might think of that did not concern him. Like a feral beast of the jungles of Huishnaveer he loped through the silent and deserted streets where the rain washed and cleansed the filth and sweating from his body. But still the red blood seeped from the gash along his temple, staining the curlish leather an angry purple.

When the time came Father Uran the Almighty would give him the strength. If only Tara's Amadis-forsaken buckles had not jammed! That was what came of selling their original solid gold buckles in order to eat, and replacing them with common metal. His own boots were laced with thongs from a forest Peloto they had stalked and killed and cooked and eaten. Such untoward misery came from the pride of a woman, even such a wild-witch girl as his sister Tara!

He heard the patrols stomping down the rain-slicked alleys, and saw the swinging lights from their lanterns. He avoided them with the instinctive skill of the jungle hunter. Used to although not relishing towns he might be; but eleven years of his first growth in savage and barbaric domains had trained him in the arts of battle and ambush, of muscle-cracking speed in death-dealing to men and beasts alike. He misliked alleys and tortuous house-bordered ways; the great avenues and squares of a mighty city he delighted in with a simple child-like gaiety of spirit that palely reflected his deep love of the open spaces of the earth. Now he ran like the shadow of nemesis towards the Keep of the Castle of Gamelon Town.

Unweaponed he might be; but that had never before stopped or hindered Torr Vorkun of Darkholm of Drugay.

Rain battered and wind lashed the Keep reared unlovely against the dark clouds. Valkur and his warriors rioted in the heavens tonight, lusting after sport and maidens and the torment of mankind. Defiant alike of the spirits of the lower worlds as of the upper, as insolent with them as with any barbarian or soldier, Torr Vorkun stared up calculatingly at the Keep.

He could charge straight in like any dull-minded barbarian hoping to seize a weapon and slay until he was pulled down; or he could try to trick the guards and talk his way in hoping to find Tara and trick his way out as a tough city-bred adventurer might do. Being the man he was, Torr Vorkun took the middle course. He would use trickery where it suited him and violence when all else failed. Simple blood hatred and lust for revenge could win no permanent prizes.

From the rain-blustery shadows he watched the sentries as they prowled. They held their halberds low against the wind.

No one knew when the first onslaught from the new people of Garthland would fall on them.

He waited his chance. At the right moment he lurched from the shadows in an angle of the walls, roaring a carousing song he had heard spewing from a tavern on the night of their first arrival here. In the rain-drenched darkness with the torchlight erratic and flickering his brown hair would go unremarked. Hiccoughing and laughing and singing, he staggered up to the sentry, who swung sullenly about.

'Some citizenry are lucky to be drinking this night while we poor soldiers are –'

The poor soldier said no more. He could not speak; he could scarcely breathe. Torr's great hand gripped around his windpipe and fierce eyes bored into his own.

'Now, dog, one yell and I snap your backbone like a rotten twig!'

The man's face and eyes went all greeny-yellow, there in the rain-streaked dimness.

'Tell me where the girl was taken! Speak fast, or you'll never speak again!'

By a fraction he loosened those cruel constricting fingers. His left hand caught the halberd to save it clanking against the flags.

'Gug-gug-gug. Up there – Prando the Uns-unsleeping!'

'Which window!'

A trembling arm pointed. The lit window glowed halfway up a tower – the one on the north east. Torr grunted. A climb, then, in this wind and rain. He thunked his borrowed halberd against the sentry's head and let him slip insensible to the flags. He stared about. Quietness apart from the unceasing sussuration of the rain and the slashing wind roar.

He dragged the sentry into a dark angle of wall and buttress and tossed the halberd down on top of the crumpled figure. Then he spat on his hands and hitched up his breech clout and put his fingers and toes into the first set of cracks of the unmortared wall. Had he been approaching a modern castle, or even this one from the other side, he would have had a moat and perhaps a glacis to contend with. As it was Gamelon Town squashed hard and confined between its crenellated walls. He went up hand over hand and booted feet merely kicking his body away from the stones. The muscles of his arms bulged and yet they did not knot like ropes, rather they slid and played like steel-strong cables.

A sill projected beneath the window that was his target and there, for a moment, he rested. He breathed as steadily as though he had merely walked briskly from his tent to the stream for a morning wash; the halt was to survey his next move and to spy out any sign of unwanted soldierly interest in him. He could see no one stirring on the ramparts.

He chinned himself and peered through the window. For a moment the tapers' light blinded him; then he saw a furnished chamber with strange-legged tables and chairs, trailing embroideries, and a bed. And bending over the bed an officer of the Gamelon army with, in his hand – Kastrader!

This, then, must be the ever-defiled Prando the Unsleeping. Torr cocked a knee on to the sill. He gathered himself.

Now, at his higher level, he could see who lay on the bed. He felt the red roaring madness mount into his brain and by an icy power of sheer self-control he forced it down. He was no instinct-ridden barbarian – not any longer!

Then he saw what Prando was up to – and Torr smiled!

Torr Vorkun smiled a cruel and malicious grin there in the wind-roaring rain perched outside a castle window.

For Prando had unbuckled Tara's left boot and had taken it off and had re-belted her slim ankle to the bed-post and now he was in the act of stripping off her right boot. With a single fluidly forceful movement of his shoulders and chest, Torr broke through the window and bounded into the room. He landed like a cat and immediately leaped halfway towards the startled Prando, who reared up, boot in one hand, Kastrader in the other.

On the bed, Tara lay completely naked.

'Well?' roared Torr joyously.

'Yes, brother mine!' she flashed back at him.

As always there came the abrupt sensation of brilliant heat and diminishing cold, a supernal flash of etheric potence noticeable only by senses outside the five known to the corporeal body.

24

Then brother and sister looked down and laughed at the little black mouse which ran and scuttled and cheeped about the castle chamber.

On the floor where the mouse had run lay a long curlish-leather boot with its buckles bent back, and the good broad-sword Kastrader.

The mouse ran to hide beneath a chair and to stare up with brilliant frightened black eyes, its whiskers twitching.

'I was quick with him,' said Tara, stepping magnificently off the bed and picking up her sword. 'I did not stop to spell it all in full force. But I spelled him good.'

'How long?'

'Half an hour, three quarters perhaps. I was over hasty with the Gnurlish-bait oaf.'

'May Valkur make sport with his spirit this night!'

'He ripped my clothes up – I can scarcely cover myself. Still – it will serve.'

Quickly Tara of Darkholm slipped on her slashed tunic, somehow rewound and tied her breechclout. Her long tanned legs slid easily into the curlish leather boots. She fingered the buckles.

'Better I had forgotten my vanity, Torr, as you suggested.'

'Forget that now. We have a climb down before us. Mayhap you'd best sling your boots over your shoulders.'

They took thier reunion casually, did these two. One glance for his head had told Tara the story of that desperate wound that was no fatal blow. Now she put her fingers gently on his temple, intoned a few simple spells of healing, massaged gently.

Torr smiled. 'Thank you – brother. My head is clear.'

'Good. Let us go.'

With Lycheaper back in its worn scabbard he felt once more a fighting man equipped by civilisation. He had enjoyed, for a few blood-red moments, the reversal to the days when he had fought as a beast.

'I think,' he said, with the image of his sister and of the in-dignities she had suffered vividly in his mind. 'I really do think we should leave a little gifting for them to remember us by.'

She kindled at once.

'What do you suggest?'

'This place is foul. It needs cleaning. And fire was ever a good cleanser.'

She nodded, impishly.

They began to pile the embroidered cloths on to the bed, puffing them up into a great glowing heap of gilt threads and silver cords, of velvets and satins. They did not think to take any to cover their own simple tunics and breachclouts. Not from this place, would they descend to take borrowed plumage.

A taper tossed into the bundle, another, and another, and soon a tiny tongue of flame spat cheerily from a gossamer shawl.

Torr nodded.

'That is good. Now we can go with lighter hearts.

The flames crawled across the precious fabrics. Smoke began to lift and permeate the room with a charred stench.

'Now, brother,' said Torr to his twin sister Tara, 'Do you go first. The climb is easy; but there may be those who would seek to delay us. You can jump on their heads if they be below. If they are above – '

'Shall I take my clothes off?'

He shook his head. 'No. I will deal with them.

He peered cautiously from the smashed window. As far as he could see no guards ventured into the pelting rain.

'Right. Down you go.'

She turned back to glance once more at him, did Tara of Darkholm, all love and affection in her eyes – and –

'Valkur! *Torr! Look!*'

He did not turn about as an ordinary man might have done. Like a springing tiger who can twist in mid-leap he sprang sideways and about and before his feet hit the floor Lycheaper flamed in his hand.

Over the bed the flames and smoke rose and coalesced and writhed. Costly silks and gossamers flared and their dying smoke spiralled upwards. And that smoke clotted and thickened and took on form and substance. Terror tugged at Torr of Darkholm then, a terror his tense muscles and ready blade would have none of, that he shrugged away as a mighty mountain peak shrugs away the snows of winter in roaring avalanches.

'Father Uran the All-mighty!'

He could not move his sword. He could not move his feet. Ragingly defiant and determined to fling himself on that blasphemous shape emerging as the smoke coalesced he could not move a single muscle.

At his side Tara remained as though petrified.

And – shrouded in smoke like clotted spider-silk the huge face and demoniac eyes of a shape from the netherworld grew and bloated and thickened. Now a hazy pentacle formed from whirls of smoke rose into view, holding and chaining the form within. Torr saw a face that might have once belonged to a frog, with gleaming jewelled eyes and scarlet horns rising above, but that face had been dead a thousand years. Here and there white bone showed splinteringly through the grey-green skin where it had sloughed away. The reek of long-unburied corpses filled the chamber.

Again and again Torr Vorkun tried to hurl himself forward against the enchantments that held him in stasis; his muscles writhed like serpents of the punishment pits of far-off Vorkandalung. But he could not move an inch.

Around the decaying frog-like body of the thing resplendent robes and barbaric jewellery and embossed metals gave by their very gorgeousness a revulsion of feeling, as they emphasised the rotting horror of the thing they clothed.

'Who dares employ thaumaturgy and practice the arts reserved to the Sorcerers of Gamelon?'

The voice croaked and gurgled like ancient pulley-wheels above a decades-dry well.

Then, flashing quicksilver in her defiance and her proud upflung chin, Tara Vorkun of Darkholm spoke.

'I used my small art to show a man as he really was!'

Somewhere, barely heard, a mouse squeaked and was silent.

'You break the most solemn vows! And yet – ' Did those malefic orbs grow brighter? Did that grotesque head incline inquisitively? 'And yet – you are not of Gamelon. Your hair –'

'Aye!' roared Torr Vorkun. 'We are not of your accursed town! But free these magical bonds that hold me and I will show you what mettle –'

'Stay! Stay! I want none of your childish barbarian taunts. My master bids you come –'

Dry skin flapped around its neck and smoke coiled into and through its eyes, twining around its scarlet horns. Sere flesh draped skeletal bones. 'But first, mortal man, since you seek to prove your manhood to this woman –'

A sharp chill tanged the air with violence.

Furtive movement began about the thing's forelegs where the writhing smoke hid the bed.

'Since I may not leave the pentacle, since I must remain in thrall to my master, the Omnipotent Wizard Zirmazd the Wily, I must send my minions to test your mettle – for my amusement!'

Now Torr could see what manner of thing it was that flopped and slid from the bed. He felt himself lose all consciousness of self, all awareness of outward feeling, felt the blood course through his body as the spell of stasis lifted. He rose on to the balls of his feet and Lycheaper felt good in his hand.

From the bed, seeming to be a part of the smoke and the pit-thing and yet undulating and ravening with a life of their own, things spawned. Long, many-necked serpents, with ranked lines of fangs, and scarlet gleaming eyes, and nightmare-bred horrors from the far deeps of ancestral horror, they poured over the bed and hurled with a vile hissing on the erect figure of Torr Vorkun.

Tara yelled a blasphemous insult; but for her the stasis held. Now, this toad-thing was having sport with her brother, sending its hell-spawned minions to test him.

Lycheaper flamed .

Scaly bodies and spined necks felt the keen bite of the true blade. Using all his skill long-won in unending hours of combats, both mock and to the death, Torr slashed until the purple ichor gushing from severed serpent heads coated him with a mail of slime. The floor grew slippery. He kept his feet with the agility that had taken him over the Cargraiolf Range in dead winter where every precipice hid beneath a coating of ice and the first slip would be the last. His blade flashed and cut, working with a smooth methodical economy of power. How long would the toad-thing send these writhing serpents hissing against him?

Now he was forced to hew as though scything long grass with the labourers of the village. Back and forth he raged cutting down the hissing vipers as they sought to sink their envenomed fangs into his legs and body. For he saw, now, with a fresh horror, that they were not directly attacking him. Fury and anger exploded in him. The things were making directly for Tara! They were trying to slide past his blade and reach the body of the girl!

Sweat rilled down his chest and span from his forehead as he swung the broadsword. A closing jaw nicked his thigh and now blood, too, ran down with the sweat.

And, all the time, the toad thing in its insubstantial web of smoke hissed a guttural accompaniment of evil laughter.

The door to Prando the Unsleeping's chamber snapped open. Goggle-eyed soldiers clustered there, their weapons upraised, their faces like those who gaze upon the last pits of death. But not one ventured into that chamber where a mortal man battled with cold steel against the enchanted ravenings of a familiar's conjuration.

Striking now in a continuous blur of speed Torr wedged his limber body between the serpents and his sister. Perfectly balanced as he fought he reached out his left arm and took up Tara. He felt a strange clinging treacly sensation as he dragged her feet from the floor. He held her jammed against his left side and back like a tree trunk.

'Torr!'

A reckless roaring oath escaped him. 'By the disgusting guts of Obese Rumphaldi Himself! No need to tell you to keep still now, Tara!'

He turned then, turned lithe and quick and with his merciless brand striking down the serpents as they crowded upon him, hissing and writhing. He strode through them as a bull strides through the chickens of a stable yard, scatering them, leaving a trail of battered corpses.

Straight he hurled himself at the bed. Straight at that insubstantial smoky toad-thing crouched there with its gallows laughter choking in its stringy throat!

4

Lycheaper Nicks on Iron

A triple-headed serpent monster, glittering scalily in the bewildering light, reared up before him, tried to sink its fangs into his chest and arm and leg. A single sweep of Lycheaper thrice-decapitated. As the purple ichor spouted Torr Vorkun lunged on, his slimed sword point-straight at the decaying face of the toad-thing within the pentacle.

'Careful, Torr! The pentacle! Smoke – if you break the pentacle the pit-thing will be free!'

'Aye, Tara – '

'It would be worse than these solid phantasms!'

The sword licked in over the wavering smoke of the star's nearest arm. Torr's slicked muscles held the brand firm and pointing, prepared to fight witchery and demonology, to plunge that blade into the very being of the evilly-chuckling familiar.

The gurgling laughter mocked him with its absolute assumption of all-power. He could feel insubstantial resistance slowing him. The wriggling serpents reared to slash their fangs at his sides and legs, their jewel-eyes glittering, their scarlet forked tongues darting.

'Now Father Uran the All-mighty give me strength!'

But his sword would not move. It remained as though like some simple-minded hero of the old legends he tried to thrust it through a granite mountain, fixed, rigid.

A great cry burst from his bruised lips. Again he thrust forward. The serpents' fangs clashed and struck as he kicked back frantically. He felt the first cold touch of the serpeant's tooth – and –

'Hold! In the name of Primotur of the Lightnings! Hold, I say!'

The voice quavered falteringly from the shadow, from the flame reflections, from the air, from the very smoke of the pentacle itself.

Immediately, as though they had never been, the serpents vanished. The blood ceased to flow from Torr's wounds and the flesh closed up whole and unblemished.

As though a giant flat hand had smashed into his chest and knocked him reeling he was flung back from the pentacle. He staggered. In his left arm Tara came to supple life. Kastrader flashed. Brother and sister, together, they stood prepared for the next onslaught, whether of magic or men they recked out.

'I hear you, master, and I obey.'

The creaking gallows-voice wheezed with a sullen spite.

'You were instructed to bring the sorcerer-workers to me, Lunga-Tuchulchya. Why do you so wantonly disobey your master of the shadows?' The old voice wheezed with a pitifully chronic self-pity. 'Bring them now!'

'I obey, master.'

For the Vorkuns, standing together in that shambles of a room, the sensations flowed together like fragments of a dream: a feeling of intense cold, of silence, of the swift rushing billows of night air and the imagined patter of rain, of movement. Then, in the same positions in which they had stood in the sleeping chamber of Prando, they stood now within an iron cage in another chamber. They stared about as the iron-barred door to the cage slammed shut with a resonant ring. It moved of itself.

'Torr!'

He put his arm around her waist. Together, side by side, the Vorkuns stared out on that chamber of thaumaturgy and magical lore.

Shadows hung in that stone-ribbed chamber shaped in the likeness of a human skull. From shrouded corners spider-webs disclosed tiny spidery forms and brilliant eyes. On cluttered benches they saw alembics and retorts, skulls, parchments inscribed with runes that dazzled, sigils and amethyst jars containing powders from nameless sources. All these things were familiar to the brother and sister from the workroom and laboratory of their dear foster father Vorkun the Wise. Yet here, too, there were objects of the darker knowledge, blasphemous athanors, smoking braziers over which bubbled cauldrons stinking with eldritch vapours, iron-trussed chests containing forbidden volumes or arcane law, whilst in one corner the obscene shape of the wombscrawn tree root glimmered with the milky falsity of flesh.

A horror held them in this chamber of thaumaturgical lore. Yet, bred up as they have been, they refused to allow what they saw to overwhelm their brains with fear.

'So there are the sorcerers, come to justice!'

The quavering voice again — and now this time the voice issued from a scrawny little man dressed all in purple and puce robes with archaic runes worked in silver thread, with stars and crescent moons scattered over the threadbare cloth. On his head the conical magician's hat wobbled ludicrously, as though tailored for a larger man, or for this man, Zirmazd the Wily, in his youth.

Torr Vorkun's arrogance burst forth as he stared on the necromancer.

'Do not think we fear you and your sorceries, Zirmazd the Wily! For you —'

A soft, sighing cooing interrupted with a tinkle of elfin sorrow.

'Ah! Nobly spoken, mortal! But I fear you must give up all hope now!'

They saw the dim red light from a glowing brazier reflecting from a tall, narrow golden cage, its bars each agleam like a spear of the gods .Within the cage and cramped so that her golden wings hung crookedly askew a golden maiden smiled dolorously at them. Her face that might have been that of a fair maiden of seventeen summers, showed dark-rimmed eyes, the mouth trembling with witnessed horrors.

Deeply her chest arched with massive pectoral muscles so that her small breasts hung like the rich fruit of the copolere vine in some tropic Huishnaveer jungle. Clad all in tiny downy golden feather she was, save over her stomach and breast and face, and in her eyes the exhausted look of the eternally-damned haunted them with its utter lack of hope.

'Keep silent, Ishrivara!' Zirmazd the Wily spoke fretfully.

He mumbled his yellow beard, his rheumy eyes vacant and pre-occupied and worried. 'I have enough trouble with that imp of hell Lunga-Tuchulchya without you – '

'Then release me, Zirmazd the Cruel! Let me fly back far to the westward to rejoin my kin, my family, all the friends of my youth – for I have been cooped up in this cage for more years than the rains take to wear away a mountain.'

'I will do so – the moment you lay for me the single golden egg I crave!'

Her young-seeming face shadowed over the golden hue and sorrow drooped her figure. Her wings would have moved but that the golden bars confined them too straightly.

'Never will I lay a golden egg for you to blaspheme with your devil-inspired arts! Never!'

'Then never will I release you from your cage, Ishrivara the Golden!'

Now the man who had remained silent until this moment, a man of squat appearance and red spade beard and eyes like spear-points, said: 'Give her to me, Zirmazd! I guarantee to make her lay her golden egg within a single morning after I take her!' His tongue flicked his thin lips. 'Her wings, Zirmazd – her wings!'

The golden flying girl, Ishrivara of the golden feathers, winced back against the bars of her cage.

'She cannot fly now, Quapartz. I do not believe that would move her – '

'The pain, Zirmazd, you must understand, the pain!'

Feebly, Zirmazd the Wily shook his head, the conical cap toppling so that he pushed it back with one yellow claw.

Quapartz, a fellow magician from his rune-embroidered cloak and his flat round star-spangled cap, leered at Ishrivara of the golden feathers and licked his lips.

'One day my turn will come!'

'But not´yet, Quapartz the Bloody-handed! For I am still the chief necromancer of all Gamelon!'

'For now, Zirmazd, for now.'

'And for now we must question these callow witch and warlock amateurs.' Zirmazd moved creakingly to stare broodingly on the Vorkuns. 'Do you imagine I would not know that you had been practising, here, in Gamelon Town itself?'

Before either Torr or Tara could throw back the hot challenge on their lips a charnel stench began in an uncluttered corner of the chambed where a scarlet and black pentacle glittered with inset gems from the stone floor. With a slow, and to the Vorkuns loathsome, deliberateness, the toad form of Lunga-Tuchulchya materialised from nothingness.

His jewelled hollow eyes still streamed a few last wisps of the smoke from Prando the Unsleeping's bed and his decaying frog-shape crouched with a kind of insolent familiarity.

Zirmazd the Wily sucked in his breath gauntly.

'I told you to bring them straight to me!'

'I needed a little entertainment – everything's dragging around here these days –'

'Do not forget, Lunga-Tuchulchya, that I am your master!'

'Speed the day.'

'Ho!' scoffed Quapartz the Bloody-handed. ' A fine familiar you have trained up, Zirmazd! If my Odudoombo spoke to me like that I'd prick him with Black Nargoth's tooth, by all the imps in Sintian!'

The frog-like familiar rippled his lipless mouth in a ghastly grin.

'You would not so maltreat me, master – would you?'

'You deserve no better – you're too insolent these bad days with all of Garthland moving against us.'

As though aware of when his presence was no longer tactful the monstrous toad-bodied thing began to shimmer and waver and to vanish back into his own netherworld.

'Come back, Lunga-Tuchulchya!'

A final wheezing howl soughed like the last gale of winter. 'I must see what wants Szstammiling . . .'

Only a dissipating swirl of smoke died above the pentacle.

Covering his trembling anger and his weak embarrassment, Zirmazd rounded on the Vorkuns.

'Now, and fast, your explanations!'

Proudly Tara of Darkholm lifted her chin. She lifted Kastrader as she spoke as though emphasising her words.

'A man sought to take advantage of me and I merely spelled him into his true likeness.'

35

'A mouse!'

'Aye.'

'Well, you know that is not allowed. You should have called the guard – oh, yes, I see.'

Curtly, Torr said : 'A noble guard you have here in Gamelon Town!'

'What want you with these poor peasant fools?' sneered Quapartz. 'If there is naught to do here I am going. The Prefect desires all our arts to be enjoyed to fight the Garthlanders. Their own thaumaturgical lore cannot match our own, founded as it is on five centuries of research; but we must work, brother-warlock! We must strive!'

'Yes, we must strive,' sighed Zirmazd the Wily. He watched with pouched lack-lustre eyes as the blocky confident form of Quapartz the Bloody-handed strutted from the skull-shaped chamber. When he had gone the old wizard let his shoulders slump. He looked at the Vorkuns in their iron cage.

'You will fare ill here.'

'We have faced worse before and will no doubt, all in the pleasure of Father Uran the All-mighty, fare worse again.'

'You call on one whose Name I do not know – ' Zirmazd's voice trailed as he shuffled to the bench and began to lift the heavy parchment pages of a tome. He muttered to himself as he laboriously turned the stiff browned leaves.

'Upopher, there is Uranil the Cursed, and, see here, Udox-trobius the Gallowed – I remember him – and Usonius the Pious – a poor, long-forgotten spirit, him – and, ah! here we are! Urang the Black Destroyer –'

'No!' shouted Torr, quite unable to decide whether to curse or to laugh.

'Uh? Oh – what name did you say? There are so many, you see, and some must repeat themselves if only by the demon-driven laws of chance. Was it not Urang the Black Destroyer?'

'By the slithering tentacles of Chomath the Defiled! It matters not to you, warlock, on whose name I called. You would do well to unlock this iron cage and let us go free.'

An unfelt gust of air blew fumes from the brazier into Zirmazd's rheumy eyes and he coughed and wiped the backs of his yellow claw hands over his face, the tears standing on his cheeks like milky eggs of the nikki-nikki insects on the trunks of beorbab trees in the Forests of Zemizond.

'That cannot be.'

'Well, tell us then, wizard, from your store of arcane lore, where may we in this wide world find the Omnipotent Sorcerer Jaran the All-seeing?'

A thin fluting whistle spluttered from the bent old man in his sorcerer's robes. After a startled moment, the Vorkuns realised he was laughing.

'Jaran the All-Seeing? Aye, I have heard of him – and I can tell you, foolish peasants, that he is long dead and buried and rotted and his spirit prowls the Halls of Black Nargoth eternally seeking the rest denied to him for ever and ever.' He flung his arms into the air, the sleeves of his robe slipping down to reveal skeletal wrists. 'Aiee! And his fate will be mine also! But I will not let it be . . . Ishrivara of the golden feathers will lay me a single golden egg and my great arts will work – I know they will! – and I shall be young and limber and free again as I was in the days of my youth, long and long ago!'

'Never!' sighed the soft whisper from the golden cage.

He screeched wildly at the golden flying girl then, his thin old face twisted into demoniac rage and despair.

'After all the years spent in the service of Tremineds and of Black Nargoth, thus to be cut off! The Prefect will cut me down and all my arts will not save me if I cannot find a sure way of holding the new people from Garthland! Aiee! My old bones ache and my poor head whirls – and all my arts and my blasphemous books of thaumaturgical lore are as nothing – and my familiar, the toad-spirit Lunga-Tuchulchya, mocks me and seeks to throw off my yoke as his master. Truly, are the evil days come upon Gamelon!'

With characteristic intolerant hewing to his path, Torr Vorkun of Darkholm rapped out : 'That is nothing to me, old man. I do not believe that Jaran the All-seeing is dead! That cannot be! By the gout-fanged foot of Obese Rumphaldi Himself! Father Uran the All-mighty would not allow it! He would not! He would not!'

'Whoever your gods are, young man, they are fallible like anyone else's. Once, long and long ago, there ruled over the

37

heavens of this land, which was not called Gamelon then, the puissant sky god Primotur of the Lightnings – he who now resides only within the confines of this chamber and the largesse of my familiar's bounds – and yet, he, too, was dethroned and cast down and chained forever in the vasty ice-caverns of Black Nargoth. For my gods, Tremineds the Supernal and Black Nargoth and all their lesser gods and goddesses clustered about them, drove the old gods from this land – and Primotur of the Lightnings may flash and spurt his fire across the heavens no more. For ever and ever he lies chained in the ice caverns, and only I, and my familiar, have access to him.'

He rambled and prowled his chamber where the smoky glow of the brazier sent crazy shadows whirling on the grimed stone walls and the golden glints from the cage and the feathered body of Ishrivara the golden feathered cut witcheries of light into the gloom.

Tara Vorkun of Darkholm clashed her true sword Kastrader against the bars of their cage.

'Almost, Zirmazd the Wily, almost I could feel it in my heart to pity you!'

'Aye, almost, peasant girl, for no man or woman born can help me now.'

'And,' put in Torr Vorkun with his steely purpose unblunted : 'That beast magician Quapartz the Bloody-handed will have your hide fried up on a griddle before many moons are out!'

'Aiee! Aiee! His spells grow stronger as his blood warms, whilst my blood chills and runs thin!'

Torr glanced at Tara. She nodded.

'We've about run him ragged now,' she said, softly.

'I think I can smash the lock with Lycheaper – it may nick the edge; but that would be a small price.'

'That poor girl with the golden feathers –'

'Yes. Her wings will be cramped.'

'I wonder just where in this world she comes from.'

Once she can fly we'll never find out –'

'Good luck to her, then, poor thing.'

Torr took a firm grip on his sword, a solid bashing hold unsuited for the fierce yet nimble sword fighting he usually practised. He measured up the swing he would need to smash the lock at a blow. At his side Tara tensed, ready, Kastrader firm and unwavering.

'My poor bones – my sere skin – they will shrivel and smoulder on the fires of Qupartz the Bloody-handed!.'

'Ready?'

'Ready, brother mine.'

Lycheaper flamed in a single smashing bludgeoning cutting blow, the edge biting into the lock and hacking through the iron. Torr felt the jolt all the way up to his neck bones. The lock, sundered, clashed to the floor.

With feral bounds Torr and Tara leaped from the cage. Kastrader's point pierced the star embroidered immediately over the weakly-beating heart of Zirmazd the Wily.

'One spell, old man, one rune, one incantation – and the cold steel skewers you!'

'No! For the sake of Supernal Tremineds himself! I beseech you!'

'Hold still!' grunted Torr .'You must give use leave to depart – your sorcerer's vow on your familiar's blood that you will hurl no enchantment against us, will never again seek to harm us – swear, or by Szangkill the Archer, my sister spits you!'

'I swear! I swear! Leave me my little life left, for I treasure it as no youth can understand! I swear by the contaminated blood of Lunga-Tuchulchya my familiar, and by the Supernal Tremineds and by Black Nargoth! I swear!'

About to relax, Tara felt Torr's hard hand beneath her right elbow, cupping it, forcing Kastrader piercingly into Zirmazd's ribs.

'And, too,' said Torr with a pitiless ferocity, 'swear by Primotur of the Lightnings that you will never harm us!'

'I – I –'

'Swear!'

'Yes, yes, by Primotur of the Lightnings I swear never to harm you more!'

'So be it.'

Kastrader came away with a tiny stain of dark-brown on its tip.

Torr Vorkun, who had hunted the striped panthers of the

forest, heard the sound at his back and moved as a spring-loaded trap moves when the unwary foot touches it. Lycheaper flamed as he sprang about. The soldiers of Gamelon Town burst in, this time without that fatal hesitation, bore him down in a tidal wave of bodies. Already Lycheaper had corpse-heaped the first five men; but the others pressed the corpses down on him, smothering and suffocating. A sword hilt smashed against his head and he sagged back, dazed, Lycheaper slipping from his bloody fingers.

He heard Tara yell and saw her collapse beside him. The last thing he saw was Zirmazd's horror-stricken face.

5

Frelgar the Pragmatist

Venomously Torr Vorkun threw off that deadly blackness. He would not succumb. He scrabbled with bloody fingers for Lycheaper and an iron-studded sandal cracked sickeningly down across his knuckles. The muscles of his forearm twined and roped as he lifted that arm up, turned his hand over, grasped the foot. He pulled. The soldier collapsed in a flurry of white cloak and rolling bronze helmet.

Him Torr lifted by the foot, whirling him like a club. He smashed down the front rank of the soldiers; but the blood made his hands slippery and the man's foot slipped away. He sailed through the dank charnel-smelling air of the skull-shaped chamber to smash into and overturn the brazier.

Ishrivara of the golden feathers made no move of anxiety or fear. With that lifeless gaze she stared at the spilled smouldering coals.

Headlong Torr Vorkun dived at the pressing soldiery. His arms pulled in heads that shattered together like three-day-old eggs in the stews of Gamelon Town. He twisted arms and felt bone and sinew crack. But blows rained down on him, battering his head, his shoulders, his body. He half-fell, fought his way up again. A solid-shafted halberd lay stunningly across the nape of his neck and he jerked forward, eyes staring.

But still he would not give in.

Tara lay still and lax. Kastrader flourished in the white hand of – of Prando the Unsleeping!

The dark-faced dandy with the scented red hair pranced on the outskirts of the conflict, shouting encouragement to his men.

Like a shaggy hriguara penned between the stockades, Vorkun made for Prando. He took a soldier by his puce tunic and threw him full at the officer. Prando wore a full corlon's rank badges, the golden cords around his shoulders shining as though newly-minted. Caught in those golden loops the flung soldier span away dragging Prando with him.

'Hai!' roared Torr Vorkin and set a foot pressing on Prando's windpipe.

But, as ever, sheer insensate revenge had played him false. As he stood grinding his foot into the corlon's windpipe a steel-hafted halberd sledged down on his head with a blow that drove him to his knees, all of red roaring Gorshern in his skull. When his scattered senses returned his wrists were firmly shackled behind his back and a chain dragged up from some evil-smelling and corpse-rotten well draped his body with iron links. He dragged himself as he walked, pushed and prodded forward by the guard.

Pale-faced, erect, her breasts heaving half-concealed by the corlish leather tunic, Tara walked at his side. She had been bound in almost as severe a fashion as her brother.

'They're beginning to understand us Vorkuns,' said Torr, with a twist to his split and bloody lips.

Prando the Unsleeping, his face still wearing an interesting green tinge from the booting across his windpipe, smashed a ring hand across Torr's cheek.

'Silence, carrion thung!'

Znunderbug-offal!' yelled Torr, for the sake of shouting his defiance at the order.

Prando lifted his ringed fist again.

'I don't, Prando the Unsleeping, have any cheese for you at the moment.'

And Tara Vorkun laughed with silvery mockery that started the angry blood into the dark cheeks of the corlon Prando the Unsleeping.

'You'll be sorry, bawd, by Black Nargoth, you'll be sorry!'

Their march was quickly ended as they wended through the corridors and draughty passageways of the castle of Gamelon Town from Zirmazd the Wily's chamber to the central hall of the Keep. Here by the light of torches and tapers the Prefect of Gamelon Town, Lohr Prendil, a bulky, stomachy man of

42

short temper and quick hands, surveyed them. His red hair cut to a bristle gleamed beneath the light. His dark close-set eyes and his thick and pouting lips might not have predisposed a fair-minded man against him; but Torr Vorkun of Darkholm was far from being a fair-minded man at this moment.

In that crowded hall of soldiers and prefecture officials and slaves and servants and clerks, the two prisoners loaded their chains stood as defiantly as they could before the steps of the oromax-stone chair of authority. Rich rugs draped that chair, gilding ran subtly around carven images of beasts and fabled giants and chimerae from the immortal pages of the *Nine-Ringed Fabulae*, so that to the suppliant it would seem that the Prefect, a mere office-holder in this town from the King-Elect of Gamelon, was in very truth a king himself.

He brooded down upon them now, his beringed left hand negligently toying with a goblet of warmed wine. The golden and jewelled chains loading his chest moved very slightly as he breathed. At his back a giant clad in furs and silver-gilt mail stood sombrely with his hands clasped over the black-thronged handle of a giant two-headed axe. The giant man and the giant axe typified the strength of the King-Elect's arm in Gamelon Town.

Through his weariness and dizziness Torr guessed that this midnight conclave had been called not because two waifs had been caught practising thaumaturgy, or even because they had slain a number – a considerable number, by Valkur! – of the Town Soldiery. The ever-present menace from Garthland had called this midnight meeting. And now these two, the twins from far Darkholm in Drugay, had been dragged into the presence.

The Prefect, Lohr Prendil, waved a beringed hand.

'Take the man below. Chain him well.' His dark cold eyes fastened like black leeches of the Suurglash swamps in the heart of the jungles of Huishnaveer on Tara's form and face. 'The girl pleases me. Strip her.'

Prando the Unsleeping stiffened. Quickly he advanced, halfway up the steps to the oromax-stone chair, inclined his red-polled head. He whispered.

After a few moments the bulky form of Lohr Prendil began to quiver. An expression of cynical amusement flitted across his face.

'By Black Nargoth! A mouse, you say! I'd have given an othar of gold to have seen it!'

'I did but – ' the thin high voice of Prando the Unsleeping began. The Prefect cut him off abruptly.

'Leave the girl. Take her to my quarters. I shall try her witchcraft for myself! Go!'

With his iron chains dragging ever closer to the stone flags Torr Vorkun was prodded below. Down to the dungeons they bore him, deep into the bowels of the earth beneath the castle of Gamelon Town. Metal gates clanged in resonant echoes, one after the other, as he traversed that ever-descending travail. Another corlon, older and more careworn than Prando, ordered the guard. His battered face showed no concern for his captive.

At the barred gate to his cell Torr was halted.

The corlon spoke harshly, without feeling, doing his job.

'I am the corlon Fringwil.' Adding to the ruddy flare of resinous torches a weird blue-green glow from lichens and mosses growing in crevices in the ancient stained walls highlighted his face in pastel-shades of corpse-flesh. 'I shall torture you until I have the truth about the Garthlanders from you. You cannot evade my questions. The Prefect has ordered it himself.'

'I know nothing about the Garthlanders – '

'You are strangers in our town! Look at your hair! You and the dark gods are leagued together against Supernal Tremineds – '

'By the swag-belly of Obese Rumphaldi Himself! I tell you I know nothing of this. We came up from the south east, from far from here – '

'The south east you say? I will soon find out if you are telling the truth. By the morning I will have spoken to the Prefect again – he will know – assuredly, he will know.'

All Torr wanted to do now was put his head down and sleep. He could feel the rumble in his belly.

'For the sake of Gitanji the Gourmet,' he said, not really

44

hoping. 'Have you some food to stop my guts from slopping into my boots?'

'Food? What need you of food? The rack and the wheel, they will nourish you!'

The iron gate slammed in his face and, off balance, loaded with manacles and chains, he toppled with a crash to the stone floor. The blue-lichen likht span about his head.

The tramp of iron-studded sandals retreated up the passage.

'Greetings, fellow unfortunate.' The voice came soft and clear from the farthest corner where moss had been stripped away to leave a shroud of shadows. 'Frelgar the Pragmatist bids you welcome to this happy abode.'

'A prankster, eh?' snapped Torr. He lay where he had fallen, twisting a little to ease the chafe of the chains and find a place where they did not gouge into his tough-thewed body.

'No, my son. I am a Pragmatist.'

'I've never heard – oh, what does that matter. Is there any way out of here?'

A light laugh. 'You do not wish to share my hospitality?'

'Why should I? Who are you? Come out into the light – if you dare!'

'Oh, I dare. I dare much. For I, too, stranger, do not have red hair.'

'Ah!'

'What is your name?'

Proudly, Torr said: 'I am Torr Vorkun of Darkholm of Drugay!'

'Oh? Methinks you ladle the titles and the places on a trifle too thickly. Do I detect the note of uncertainty? Two places of origin? Two names?'

'By Valkur! You try me, stranger!'

'That I would, and gladly. But I am forsworn to all that nonsense. Once, not so long ago, I was a wizard in good standing – but not here, not in accursed Gamelon Town. But now I am a Pragmatist – I am voluntarily an unfrocked sorcerer!'

'A what?'

'An unfrocked sorcerer.'

There, in the dismal dungeon below the castle of Gamelon Town, Torr of Darkholm laughed.

'An unfrocked sorcerer! Now I have the tale from beyond the world's rim!'

'Voluntarily, Torr whatsit, voluntarily, mind!'

'If you were once a sorcerer, you must have your knowledge still. Spell us out of here! Strike off these chains! Free us by enchantment so that I may seek out the Prefect and strip the flesh from his bones!'

'And a very bloodthirsty ambition that is, to be sure. But I am defrocked by personal choice. I no longer practise.'

'You no longer practise.'

'Just so.'

'And may I be allowed to see this wonder of the world?'

The sound of laboured breathing, the shifting of straw, was followed by a tiny chingle of chain. A man moved into the lichen-light.

Once he had been wearing a white tunic trimmed with woce-loan fur, and black cloak with a triple cape and fur-trimmed hood. Now the rags tattered glumly about his short hardy body with the marks of old scars wealing the ribs. His hair – his hair showed still traces of a darker brown than Torr's own light brown thatch through the iron grey poll. Straight and clipped to the neck, his hair marked him as a foreigner. A sudden warming gush of friendship for this man engulfed Torr then – irrationally, to his way of thinking.

Frelgar's face showed the mark of years in the lines about his dark blue eyes and firm-lipped mouth. His nose had been broken at some time and now jutted slightly adrift. He gave Torr the impression of an old well-worn pewter jug that had served its drinking master well and was now affectionately filled with water instead of wine.

'So you're Frelgar, the so-called Pragmatist.'

'I have that honour.'

'And you are unable to get us out of here?'

Frelgar did not answer directly. Instead, he said : 'There is a time in the affairs of men for gods and sorcerers and there is a time for men to face the awful dark alone. I preach the reliance of mankind on mankind.'

'You have chosen a noisome den for your sermon.'

'Alas, Torr What-have-you, the choice was not mine.'

46

'Stay!' said Torr heatedly. 'I mislike your slighting reference to my name —'

'Then put my cynical mind at ease, my son.'

'I was raised by a good kind man, a foster father, Vorkun the Wise, and his name in love and loyalty I took for my own —'

'You did not know your parents?'

Angrily, feeling the irrational barbarian shame strong on him, Torr shook his head. 'My sister and I were abandoned on the doorstep of Vorkun's mountain cave. We lived wild, among the beasts of the jungle and the terrors of the snows, there around the Cargraiolf Range until we were eleven years old.'

'And?'

'I do not know why you can make me tell you these old things, Frelgar the Pragmatist. Some whispered, when we entered Darkholm, that Vorkun was our natural father; but he denied this with tears in his eyes — he sorrowed for that, for, mark me, Pragmatist, he would have been proud to have been our natural father!'

'I'm sure. So after you fought your way to control of Darkholm —'

'How could you know that?'

Frelgar spread his supple hands. 'I have experience of this world far beyond the bumpkin confines of Gamelon March. I know a man when I see one. So Darkholm —'

'Darkholm is my steading! A great stone house, with panelled walls and many windows, with a strong watch-tower and an iron-barred gate —'

'You must must have your troubles, then, in Drugay.'

'Aye! Sometimes there are Gnurlish raids —'

Frelgar sighed. 'When I was a youth I could not keep my nose out of books of alchemycal lore. I could conjure a rabbit spirit when I was nine — but I wander.'

A harsh laugh spat from Torr Vorkun. 'I wish we could wander, Frelgar, far away from this foul pest hole.'

'You cannot break your chains?'

The links smoked with rust as Torr strained.

'No,' he gasped at last, the sweat standing out on the filth griming his forehead and arms. 'They defy me —'

'They must be strong, at least, then. Here.' He shuffled

closer with a clang of fetters. 'I have been here longer and they know my strength is not as yours. Try mine.'

Now Torr put out all his strength. His teeth clamped together and the sinews of his neck stood out like veins of granite between rain-washed limestone. He strained. He felt the direct mocking challenge from this unpredictable unfrocked wizard. He exerted the strength that had grown in his back and legs and arms during those years of barbarism and pulled with unremitting force. And, also, using the cunning skills of his days as a man of civilisation he tugged skilfully at one single link he judged weaker than the others, straining and levering and bending and stretching, until –

Pingg!

With a great gasp Torr Vorkun of Darkholm flung the shattered chains from Frelgar the Pragmatist.

'Now may mankind sleep easier!' Frelgar massaged his wrists tenderly. 'Never have I met the man with strength unto your, Torr Vorkun of Darkholm of Drugay!'

Torr laughed.

'So sheer muscular strength impresses you, little man?'

'My son, I am not as young as I once was. A strong arm and sinews of steel are aye comforting to me now.' He swallowed and wiped his lips. 'And I respect your name – '

'Would you respect the name the barbarians with whom I learned the primitive arts of war gave me? The barbarians among whom I wandered until I was grown enough to take Darkholm for myself – that name?'

'What name was that, my son?'

'*Torr the Slayer!*'

'I see. My stomach is strong – '

Remembering those days, Torr grunted; but did not comment further. He felt a respect for hidden strengths in this man.

They talked a little more, desultorily; but very soon the great weariness in Torr overcame him so that he slept.

The voice shocking into his brain brought him instantly awake. He had no idea how long he had slept; the blue lichen-light played as eerily and steadily as ever. He tried to spring up and the chains dragged him back.

'*Torr!* The Prefect refuses – the Black Bodice – Torr!'

And then – blankness, silence, emptiness.

Torr Vorkun shook there in the dank pits below the castle of Gamelon Town. His great fists knotted as he lifted his arms against the constricting chains.

'What ails thee, my son?'

'My sister – she is in trouble! And I cannot hear her voice – something has happened!'

Frelgar the Pragmatist did not make a single hesitation over Torr's word. He accepted them. He well knew – who better? – of the power latent in the human mind. All the sorcerers of Fabled Khorsakand could not, hoped and prayed Frelgar, stand against the might of a single man's own faith.

On the echoes of Torr's voice the oncoming tramp of iron-shod feet boomed and clanged down the passageway.

'It is the corlon Fringwil. He has come to take you away and put you to the question!'

Genuine alarm and fear showed in Frelgar's shrewd eyes.

The gated door thrust wide.

'Come with us, peasant outlander! Now you will see what song the wheel and the rack will make you sing!'

6

The Axe of Murgur

The corlon Fringwil had brought six guards with him because Torr, the peasant overlander, was so heavily chained. That, reasoned a normal man, would be enough.

But Torr Vorkun of Darkholm had been refreshed by a deep sleep. Despite the hollow rumbles from his belly he felt the sure strength flowing in his arms and legs. He braced those corded legs wide as the six guards advanced with levelled halberds. His wild barbarian instincts marshalled and directed by his cunning martial brain selected targets and measured strength and weakness.

As the corlon stood aside within the doorway and the guards prodded forward, he shouted, hard and high: 'Now, Frelgar!' and flung himself forward in a thrashing smother of chains.

The first two men went down without a sound.

The second two, halberds darting, tried to spear his swinging arms. A length of chain like the ancient mace of Moray laid open one fellow's scalp. Torr bit a bight of chain around the second'd neck and gave enough leverage to snap the spinal cord with a crack lost in the horrified shouts of the other guards. He plunged on without stopping.

'Spear him down, you fools!' yelled Fringwil.

He snatched out his curved scimitar, all blued steel and runneling red in the lichen-light and the torches' flare.

A halberd snapped as Torr put one foot on it, pressing its owner back. He snapped the chain across the man's throat and swung towards the last guard. This man had jumped back to give his halberd clearance and now he drove the point hard at the bundled mass of chains and brawny muscularity raging in the cell.

The point scored Torr's ribs through the intertwining chains. He ignored the sudden razor-like pain and swung a loose loop of chain, bunched into an iron mace. The guard dodged and drove in again – and fell back screaming as a halberd thrust under Torr's arm and took him clean in the throat, ripping his neck asunder.

'Thanks, Frelgar!'

'By Black Nargoth! I do not believe my eyes!'

But the corlon Fringwil had to believe, with Frelgar's halberd point at his throat and the clumsily knotted flail of chain swinging menacingly from Torr's sinewy fist.

After that Frelgar took only a few moments to find the iron keys to release the chains. He took them from Fringwil's gold-laced tunic with ungentle fingers. Instead of using them to release Torr to the torch-lit terror of the torture room, Fringwil had been instrumental in freeing Torr to the dim blue-lit liberty of the dungeon and the corridors of the castle.

'Now I know how Amadis must have felt, when she threw off the Dragon yoke!' exclaimed Torr, stripping the links from his body.

'Oh, aye,' grumbled Frelgar. 'Legends, legends. When will you children have had enough of them?'

'Not for aye and aye, I hope and trust!' replied Torr with an acerbity that brought an answering tightness to Frelgar's lips.

'And this one?' he asked with a lift of an eyebrow.

Torr took Fringwil's curved scimitar and hefted it.

'A fancy blade, suited for fine work but of little use in the fray. It will serve.'

Fringwil eyed his own sword stonily. He did not flinch. 'If you must kill me now foreigner, then make it quick.'

'Like this?' shouted Torr, on a sudden, and brought the hilt down with a thudding blow on Fringwil's head. The corlon collapsed. Not intending to kill but only to stun. Torr did not bother to examine the corlon; it made little difference to him if the man lived or died. 'Let us go!' he said, and a joyous exuberance boiled up within him.

They used the corlon's keys to unlock the serried gates, not stopping to relock them. Through the underground passage-ways they made their way up towards the castle keep.

'The vanity of men!' sighed Frelgar the Pragmatist. 'You had four halberds to choose from – yet you took the fancy sword!'

'I know weapons,' replied Torr quietly. 'I doubt there is a weapon in this world I could not handle. I chose for other reasons than pride.'

'Hah!' snorted Frelgar; but he did not press the argument.

Twice Torr struck silently and shrewdly, catching the limp bodies of guards and lowering them to the flags. They prowled on until they reached a narrow door that let in brilliant sunlight and a strange smell that Torr, with relish, decided must be what Gamelon Town called fresh air.

'By Gitanji the Gourmet!' he growled. 'What I could do to a haunch or two with spiced gravy and crumbled pastry!'

'We left the torture chamber below,' said Frelgar dryly.

'I knew you were a prankster – hush! Over there, beside that stone doorway –'

'I see.'

More and more Torr was coming to have a firm confidence in this quiet-spoken unfrocked sorcerer. A certain steely self-centred purpose in him answered that in Torr. Over by the stone doorway three guards lounged, their halberds loose, their faces slack with morning boredom. Their sandals scuffed the stone flags idly.

Those three – they went down as the sapling goes down before the breath of the winged horses of Valkur and his warriors as they ride the storm clouds. Torr looked about.

'This way,' said Frelgar confidently. 'There is but one gate-way between us and the inner street. Once we can reach the alleys of this stinking town we can lose ourselves, hair or no hair.'

'Do you go on, friend Frelgar. As for me – this is my way.'

Without stopping to see what Frelgar would do Torr began to lope around the base of the wall. He headed directly for the side door inset below the grand stair that led up to the main entrance. Up there more guards lolled, killing time on watch,

looking out, and not down into the well below the stairway.
'Torr!'

Vorkun took no notice. He went on. And on his face a look that – could the Prefect Lohr Prendil or Prando the Unsleeping have seen – would have scared them liver-white.

'What are you doing, Torr – this is the way to freedom!'

Torr Vorkun reached the door below the stairs. It opened to his hand. Within, light streaming down from arrow-slits at ground level showed him stairs up. Up she went, padding, silent, the scimitar in his fist curved and ready.

To few ears outside a jungle killing area would the sound at his back have brought any response. But to Torr Vorkun those almost silent footfalls told eloquently of the unfrocked sorcerer, unwillingly following him. He made no comment.

They reached the floor in this gate tower that would lead them into the gallery above the great hall of the keep. A few torches guttered from the night in brass beckets. Doorways stood open, some with embroidered curtains still drawn. A silence lay on this place – the early morning silence when a castle gives over from breaking its fast and measures itself against the tasks of the day.

Torr lowered his rumbling voice.

'D'you know where the Prefect's quarters are – or must we seize a wight and wring it from him?'

Frelgar pointed. 'I know. He – questioned me there.' He grimaced. 'In the south-east tower.'

Cautiously they crossed the gallery over the great hall. Below them slaves – poor beaten creatures whose badge of servitude lay in their black or yellow or brown hair – washed and polished and cleaned. Soldiers clustered in doorways. Outside the high shrilling of dryness reached them as ostlers plied their trade. The mounting bustle of a castle day increased in tempo, sluggishly, for the castle of Gamelon Town was an old and fragile structure.

Up the stairs of the south-east tower they ascended and three times Torr struck and three times they lowered the senseless guards to the treads.

Outside an oaken door with brazen rivet heads and carven

animals and outlandish beorbarb leaves Frelgar halted. A sly smile curved his firm lips.

'I shall admonish myself later for what is to happen now; but for now – I relish it!'

Torr had no time for such niceties. He shouldered the door open, skewered the captain of the guard who swung about, sheep-faced, and strode into the chamber. Like unto Prando the Unsleeping's chamber it was, yet vaster, more gorgeous, more cumbered with costly silks and embroideries and golden and ivory statues and fans of peacock feathers.

Lohr Prendil, the Prefect, was washing himself in a silver bowl supported on a silver tripod and the lavastone fell from his hands to splash with a rich tinkle into the water. He goggled. His vast bed with the drawn up curtains of red velvet dominated all one wall of the chamber. There, as he had not expected, Torr did not see Tara. He looked about fiercely, the scimitor dropping bright blood to the intricately-woven colours of the Shandascrine rugs. A curtained alcove – movement? soft breathy breathing?

He left the Prefect to Frelgar's exacting halberd and strode across the chamber, ripped the curtain away.

Standing enclosed in an iron cage shaped by cunning hinges to the form of her body, an iron wedge in her mouth, iron spikes pressing whitely against her flesh, Tara Vorkun stared defiantly back at him.

As she recognised who it was her reserves of strength rushed together and Torr saw her little body sag against the iron spikes. Puzzled, he looked closer. Around her waist, flaring to the swell of her hips and cupping her breasts, a black garment encinctured her. Some strange sheen of that material, a sliding greenish-black-rust hue, made his eyes smart as he started at it.

He went back to the Prefect and took him by the scruff of the neck from under Frelgar's halberd point. He carried him like a butcher carries a woceloan carcass to the furriers.

'Release her, Lohr Prendil – now!'

Gobbling, the Prefect bent to the springs binding the hinges. The cage snapped open, and Tara staggered forward to fall into Torr's crooked left arm. Her mouth showed bloody bruises yet, in that glory of the moment, she contrived a small smile for her brother.

'Tara – ?'

'I – I am – all right. But this – this thing – this Black Bodice!'

'I did not hear you call –'

'It is a magic woven by Quapartz the Bloody-handed. Now until it is removed I cannot work my own small sorceries, for I cannot strip myself naked. And, Torr – it stops me speaking with my mind to yours!'

'We will see about that,' said Torr Vorkun of Darkholm.

With the bloodied scimitar he cut at the top of the bodice between Tara's breasts. It resisted. Carefully, fearful lest he injure the white flesh of his sister, he prised the blade down, sawing at an angle. The material with its sinister hue resisted, would not be cut.

'Hurry!' whispered Freglar. 'I know of the Black Bodice – fitted for witches and female wizards and others of unknown sex. It will not come loose save by the intervention of a superior enchantment – and those I have –'

'Yes, I know,' snapped Torr. 'Those you have disclaimed.'

Arrogantly he thrust the Prefect within the cage and reversing Prendil's movements with the springs shut the iron spikes on him and thrust the iron wedge into his mouth so that teeth crunched and shattered.

'Now we get out of here, Frelgar, into your warren of back alleys.'

'Stand!' boomed a herculean voice.

They whirled.

The giant who had stood by the Prefecture chair in his furs and silver gilt mail bounded towards them brandishing his double-bitted axe. His broad powerful face showed an unholy joy at thus confronting axe-fodder.

'Murgur the Axe!' gasped Tara. With a gesture at once instinctive and futile her hand flew to her waist.

Frelgar howled in passionate fury, breaking the self-imposed bonds of his discipline.

'Now who was right and who wrong in weapons choice, O prideful Torr of Darkholm?'

Murgur the Axe boomed a terrible laughter as he swung the

axe over and down. Lithely Torr leaped sideways and lithely Tara leaped the other. Curved and bloody, Torr's scimitar lashed in, to grind and catch and break on silver-gilt mail!

With a stump of metal in his hand Torr faced the giant man with the giant axe.

With a fuming courage Freglar dashed in from the side, halberd low, caught the giant over the hip, span him around. With a bellow he brought the axe down, missing Freglar but splintering the halberd haft to kindling.

'Quits in weapons, good Frelgar!'

Weaponless, the three faced the axeman, warily, backing away, hands spread, their eyes concentrating on every bunching of muscle, on every sudden eye-movement.

He made a dart at Tara, span, quickly, swung down on Frelgar who squeaked and all rabbity-hoppitty toppled over a chair and went down in a flurry of silks and laces. Torr jumped in and smashed a fist into the giant's nose. Red blood spouted; but Murgur shook it away and swung again, raging, the axe a shimmering arc about his head.

All tumbled as he was Frelgar thrust out a filthy foot with the dungeon straws still lodged between the toes. Murgur of the Axe hooked an ankle and went down. Savagely Torr beat a fist at the giant's nape but the blow caught a muscled shoulder, staggering Murgur lopsidedly into the remnants of the chair. Like a crazed hriguara in rut he bounded up again. His broad face now showed a tinge of surprise. These three had not yet tasted the cleaving power of his axe – and this puzzled Murgur of the Axe mightily.

'Circle him!' rapped Torr.

Scrabbling frantically, Frelgar staggered away to one side as Torr tried to draw the giant on. He skipped the axe blade, leaped in, feeling his hollow stomach rebel, smashed a blow into Murgur's belly. The axeman whoofed but brought the axe up again.

Over by the alcove between the un-castle-like wide windows, Tara saw a stand of arms against the drapes. Weapons glinted there, an edge here, a point there, catching reflections of the sunlight that streamed in on either side of the stand.

She reached out – selected – snatched – whirled.

56

'Torr!

In the act of sliding a glancing blow of the axe that would have jellied a lesser man's brains, Torr Vorkun heard his sister's call. He pivoted, stuck up a hand, aimed to cup the end of that spinning glinting silvery trajectory that flew from his sister's hand to his own. He felt the solid thump of wound silver wire in his palm.

Lightly he rose on to the balls of his feet, swinging in to face the roaring form of Murgur the Axe.

Lycheaper flamed.

'Now, giant of znunderbug-offal! Defend yourself!'

Murgur opened his mouth to bellow an obscene answering challenge, the axe swishing like typhoon rain through standing corn, and Lycheaper flamed in with two deft sundering strokes, and Murgur the Axe stood looking stupidly as the axe and his right arm fell all bloody to the floor, and looked no more as his head lolled from his shoulders.

'By the mercy of man!' exclaimed Frelgar. 'Now I know why you are called Torr the Slayer!'

Tara lifted Kastrader from the weapons rack.

'There is also a bow here, brother mine.'

'We must hurry!' Frelgar fretted. 'Someone will surely have discovered a sentry not at his post by now – the torture room ghouls – the guards on the stairs – '

'Yes, yes, friend Frelgar. But we cannot leave like this. Quickly now! Clothe yourselves. And, Frelgar, I take it you can handle a sword as well as a halberd!'

'Aye!' Frelgar might have spoken surlily had he not been a Pragmatist. 'But not all swords are as yours – '

'That is true.'

While Tara hunted for clothes, Torr washed the blood and filth from himself in Prendil's silver bowl. He felt a trifle more human – and kept that weakening feeling under control in his present wild circumstances. He examined the bow. Built of laminated ram's horn, with reinforcements of dragobrane horn, he judged by the coiled amber colour, the bow held a powerful pull, singing to the cord.

Frelgar said: 'I doubt if I could have strung that bow; yet you did it without putting it beneath your knee.'

'A knack. Ah, friend Frelgar, and a natty outfit, indeed!'

For Frelgar had found a shining white tunic, trimmed with bullion, and over it had flung a wide black cloak trimmed not with woceloan fur like his own tattered rag; but with good ermine, gleaming in the early sunshine. Tara donned one of Prendil's hunting outfits, green, loose around her waist and tight over her chest.

'There is no time to band my breasts, as usual, Torr. If the thing splits when I swing Kastrader, so be it.'

Prendil had nothing that would fit Torr; but he slit up, with Tara's help, the sides of a fawn hunting tunic. With his own dragobrane leather belt strapped around it it served as a kind of tabard.

He slung a full quiver of arrows over his back, thrust the strung bow alongside.

'Take yourself a sword, then, Frelgar.'

'Very well. But I think I will retain this halberd habit — ' He let his firm lips curve into his sly smile as he took a hafted weapon from the wall.

'We would not take anything from Prando's chamber; but now our circumstances are different.' Torr looked about on his little company. He kicked the heap of discarded corlish leather with the rips and the blood disfiguring it.

He bent, picked up Murgur's axe. The black-thonged haft fitted his palm. He swung it twice, thoughtfully.

'Cloaks,' he said.

Dark wine-coloured cloak for Tara, dark midnight-blue cloak for Torr. Shrouded, their weapons half-concealed, they prepared to leave the chamber — and then Torr Vorkun paused.

In the fight a chest had spilled and from its brass-bound oak bright coins splashed spots of colour in the sunlight.

'For the lack of these — and that dratted chicken — all this began,' he said. 'I no longer have need of stealing — I have never stolen, for Darkholm was — was — '

'Darkholm is ours!' flashed Tara.

'Aye! And at the level we are now, taking enough money for our wants is not stealing — it is hardly recompense for our suffering and the indignity heaped on you, my sister. Rather, we establish our contempt for these lordling curs of Gamelon Town!'

'Truly,' said Frelgar the Pragmatist. 'And it is mighty useful on the journey through life!'

They took a bag of gold each.

They left that chamber where Murgur of the Axe lay bereft of good right arm, of head, and of axe.

They quitted that lair where Lohr Prendil, the Prefect, suffered in his cage of iron with the iron wedge jammed into his mouth.

'Down!' said Frelgar confidently.

But Torr Vorkun led off, after they had reached the rampart level, towards Zirmazd's tower. Tara followed.

'What?' yelped Frelgar. 'What foolery now? The place will be a midden of flies wearing puce and bronze any moment!'

The castle of Gamelon Town, three centuries old, had been built with the keep as part of the outer walls in the fashion of that time in this part of the world, with the main gate adjoining with its small and insignificant barbican pressed against the houses of the town. Along the ramparts, crouching below the merlons, the three ran. The black cloak, the wine-dark cloak and the midnight-blue cloak, swirling with the speed of their going, they ran towards that evil tower of sorcery.

'You're mad, mad!' gasped Frelgar.

Now beneath them in the ward a clamour arose. The sound of yelled orders, of startled oaths, of the clangour of weapons, rose unmistakable as a grim warning. They ran on.

'They know we've broken out!' yelped Frelgar. 'Why did I listen to you, you maniac! I should have gone when I had the chance!'

'There is no chance of breaking through the soldiery now, Frelgar! No way out of their castle now!'

'Aiee! Don't I know it! I have doomed myself by following you – Torr Vorkun of somewhere beyond reason!'

'Torr – what now?' Tara ran fleetly beside her brother, untroubled if he showed unconcern.

'We would never reach the gateway alive. They would shoot us down –'

'Oh, my poor old bones, that they should be thus broken for the sake of a barbarian madman with a sword!'

'Quiet, Frelgar my friend. There is one chance – one single slender chance. Where we are going – to the skull chamber of Zirmazd the Wily – there lies our hope!'

7

Constriction

'Zirmazd the Wily?'

'Oh, oh – I should live to be carrion thung's meat !'

Harshly, bashing open Zirmazd's door, Torr chuckled.

'You do not fool me, Frelgar the Fighter !'

Zirmazd the Wily had not slept well. He started up as three cloaked figures burst in, weapons in their hands, their eyes coals of energy and hate.

'What – what?'

Then he recognised them, and his weak old heart thumped within him like the unborn foetus of the fabled psaurobrinth that flies from its mother's womb full fledged from the moment of birth.

Instinctively his hands flew up and he began to intone an incantation that might have blighted them where they stood or transmogrified them into worms or banished them to the ice caverns of Black Nargoth to dwell in eternal damnation chained beside Primotur of the Lightnings.

'Hold, wizard !'

Torr strode in, looking keenly about, seeing no one apart from Zirmazd and the trapped and lonely figure of the golden feathered girl.

'Remember your sworn oath ! If you harm us now – what will be your fate?'

Zirmazd trembled. 'And this man?'

Frelgar – Frelgar the Pragmatist swelled. He moved forward firmly, blocky, grey-haired, proud.

'I know you, Zirmazd the Fumbler !'

'What?' Zirmazd's yellow clawed hands trembled at his mouth. 'How know you that name, that old blasphemous name?'

'Once I, too, followed your loathsome trade. But now I am a free man, untroubled by your guilt, a voluntarily unfrocked sorcerer – voluntarily, mind!'

Zirmazd nodded shakily, his rheumy eyes glinting. 'Then I can do nothing against you –'

'Just so.'

'Now, Zirmazd,' snapped Torr. 'You will summon your obnoxious familiar!'

'What!' gasped Tara. Then, comprehending, she laughed her delighted silvery chuckle. 'How appropriate!'

'I have promised that no harm shall come to you through me.' Zirmazd tried to earn back the reputation of his name. He had not been called Wily just to obliterate that old cruel name of Fumbler. 'But I made no promise to aid you. I shall call through my summoning arts the soldiers – Prando the Unsleeping – they will take you. You cannot escape!'

Torr laughed in his face. He strode to the golden cage and a single blow from Lycheaper shattered the soft golden lock. He pried the gate open.

'Not so, Zirmazd the Foolish! Do you forget Quapartz – Quapartz the Bloody-handed? How say you – what would he do if the soldiers found us here, unharmed in your chamber? Would he not wonder why? He would think you had aided us. He would question. Prendil – him of the iron gag – would rage no less viciously at you than us! Cease to summon the soldiers – or you burn on Quapartz's fires!'

'By Primotur of the Lightnings! You have me in a cleft – I see, I see!'

Tara stepped swiftly to the golden cage, assisted Ishrivara of the golden feathers out. She staggered and Tara's supple arm caught her. The golden wings began to spread, falteringly, shining their golden glory hesitant.

'No!' screeched Zirmazd. 'The golden egg! All my youth and strength –'

'Peace, Zirmazd! Do you not understand that Ishrivara would never in ten thousand years lay you that coveted golden egg? Let her go free – for by Primotur of the Lightnings, if you do not I will cut you down where you stand!'

Zirmazd staggered back, one hand to his chest, the other

supporting his tottering body against an alembic-strewn bench.

'I thank you,' came Ishrivara's soft voice, faint and breathless with the wonder of the moment. 'I feel – dizzy. My wings! My poor shrivelled wings!'

'Take heart: Ishrivara of the golden feathers,' roared Torr Vorkun. 'For methinks Zirmazd is Wily enough to set us all free now.' He swung on the wizard, Lycheaper a brand of commanding steel. 'Now do you summon Lunga-Tuchulchya and direct him to set us beyond the walls of this accursed castle, and supply us with drynes ready victualled – for by Gitanji the Gourmet I could eat your shrivelled heart basted in olive oil right this minute!'

The shudder that shook Zirmazd brought that silvery tinkle of laughter from Tara and a relished response from Frelgar and brought even a tiny responsive twitching to the drawn lips of Ishrivara.

'Or, Zirmazd, does your familiar rule you these days?'

Zirmazd tried to draw himself up, pushing at his toppling conical cap, weakly wrathful.

'My familiar knows who is master. By the foul intestines of Black Nargoth – I'll prick him with Nargoth's tooth, so help me Tremineds!'

'Well – see to it, now!'

That familiar nauseating charnel stench drifted from the scarlet and black pentacle and the blasphemous outlines of the toad-thing from the pit began to form.

'Did soldiers see you enter here?' quavered Zirmazd.

'No, I think not. But, if they did, your great enchantments could make them think otherwise, I trust?'

'Yes, yes, I can spell a simple soldier.'

'What does my puissant master require?' The gurgling swamp-voice creaked with sarcastic venom from the pentacle.

Zirmazd told him. He finished: 'And if you attempt any pranks for your entertainment, or spill word of this to Odudoombo – or any familiar in your hell-pits – I will sting you with Black Nargoth's tooth, so help me all the imps of Sintian! Remember!'

The weak old voice must have carried a conviction to Lunga-Tuchulchya, for the frog-thing made no ironic comment. Instead he croaked a subdued : 'Yes, master. I hear and obey.'

'That is more like a faithful familiar!'

'At least, Zirmazd,' said Torr before they went, 'you can thank us for putting a little discipline into your thaumaturgical organisation.'

The wizard's enraged howl dwindled and vanished as a gulf of ice and wind and scorching heat and stillness enveloped them, whirling, end over end tumbling, until – until they stood in a stable yard under the bright morning sun with the familiar sounds and smells of dryne stables about them. Ostlers and stable boys moved about their work sluggishly. A short stout red-haired man led to dryne mares and two dryne stallions towards them. They pulled their concealing cloak-hoods tighter about their betraying hair. Ishrivara, with the magically contrived cloak, kept still.

'I have them all ready for you, good sirs,' said the stable man, not smiling, not frowning, just doing a job. 'All ready victualled and paid for and ready to go.'

They thanked him, mounted, and Frelgar tossed a golden coin, winking in the sun, to be caught by a fat red hand.

Enchantment was at work here; no one took any notice of their hot bundled cloaks in the sunshine, or of the tip of Isrivara's golden feathered wings. The magic mantle concealed.

'Thank you, good sirs. May Drygol smile on you.'

They jingled out of the stable yard and headed down the rutted road, dried already in the sun from last night's rain. The air smelled sweeter here and soon they passed beneath the town gate with a bored sentry standing still over his halberd. Torr peered closer.

'By Chomath the Defiled! That sentry is ensorcelled! Truly, Zirmazd is keeping his blasphemous word!'

'As well he might, from what I gather,' said Frelgar.

They struck straight across the road and headed out towards the Forest of Greater Stretting, in a wide-bayed artificial clearing of which stood Gamelon Town. They left the town to dwindle away beneath the warming sun. Beyond that again lay the Forest of Stretting, and the great plains, and beyond those again, far and far, over hill and dale and through mountain and swamp, lay the lands of the League of Praterxes and Paltomir

Of All Brands Sold: Lowest tar: 2 mg. "tar," 0.2 mg. nicotine
av. per cigarette, FTC Report Apr. 1976.
Kent Golden Lights: 8 mg. "tar,"
0.7 mg. nicotine av. per cigarette by FTC Method.

NEW!
KENT GOLDEN LIGHTS
LOWER IN TAR
THAN ALL THESE BRANDS.

Non-menthol Filter Brands	Tar	Nicotine	Non-menthol Filter Brands	Tar	Nicotine
KENT GOLDEN LIGHTS	**8 mg.**	**0.7 mg.***	RALEIGH 100's	17 mg.	1.2 mg.
MERIT	9 mg.	0.7 mg.*	MARLBORO 100's	17 mg.	1.1 mg.
VANTAGE	11 mg.	0.7 mg.	BENSON & HEDGES 100's	18 mg.	1.1 mg.
MULTIFILTER	13 mg.	0.8 mg.	VICEROY 100's	18 mg.	1.2 mg.
WINSTON LIGHTS	13 mg.	0.9 mg.	MARLBORO KING SIZE	18 mg.	1.1 mg.
MARLBORO LIGHTS	13 mg.	0.8 mg.	LARK	18 mg.	1.2 mg.
RALEIGH EXTRA MILD	14 mg.	0.9 mg.	CAMEL FILTERS	18 mg.	1.2 mg.
VICEROY EXTRA MILD	14 mg.	0.9 mg.	EVE	18 mg.	1.2 mg.
PARLIAMENT BOX	14 mg.	0.8 mg.	WINSTON 100's	18 mg.	1.2 mg.
DORAL	15 mg.	1.0 mg.	WINSTON BOX	18 mg.	1.2 mg.
PARLIAMENT KING SIZE	16 mg.	0.9 mg.	CHESTERFIELD	19 mg.	1.2 mg.
VICEROY	16 mg.	1.1 mg.	LARK 100's	19 mg.	1.2 mg.
RALEIGH	16 mg.	1.1 mg.	L&M KING SIZE	19 mg.	1.2 mg.
VIRGINIA SLIMS	16 mg.	1.0 mg.	TAREYTON 100's	19 mg.	1.4 mg.
PARLIAMENT 100's	17 mg.	1.0 mg.	WINSTON KING SIZE	19 mg.	1.3 mg.
L&M BOX	17 mg.	1.1 mg.	L&M 100's	19 mg.	1.3 mg.
SILVA THINS	17 mg.	1.3 mg.	PALL MALL 100's	19 mg.	1.4 mg.
MARLBORO BOX	17 mg.	1.0 mg.	TAREYTON	21 mg.	1.4 mg.

Source: FTC Report Apr. 1976
*By FTC Method

8 mg. "tar," 0.7 mg. nicotine
av. per cigarette by FTC Method.

© Lorillard 1976

KENT GOLDEN LIGHTS
ONLY 8 MG TAR.
YET TASTES SO GOOD,
YOU WON'T BELIEVE THE NUMBERS.

the Blessed under the peaceful sway of the Lord High King.

Just how far beyond that, again, lay Darkholm within the realm of Drugay they did not like to dwell on.

'We have come a long way, sister,' said Torr Vorkun.

'If what Zirmazd said, we have little way left to go.'

'Nay, Tara the silver voiced! We will find Jaran the All-seeing yet!'

Frelgar the Pragmatist jerked up his head. He would have spoken; but Ishrivara threw down the borrowed cloak that had once belonged to Zirmazd the Wily. She spread her golden wings in the sunlight. She looked like an angel from some phantasmagoria from the pages of the *Nine-Ringed Fabulae*.

'Freedom!' she lisped in that soft golden voice. 'I can scarce comprehend it . . .'

'Wings such as those should never be cramped in a cage,' said Torr Vorkun. He looked again at this feathered girl.

Slight, her body, and yet firm, with that deep pectoral development and those small rounded breasts, those long narrow thighs and dainty feet, her whole form vibrant with the power of flight, she conveyed to Torr Vorkun a dizzying sense of unearthly beauty and supernal sadness.

She stroked her wings experimentally against the morning air. Against the deep greens of the forest they shone bravely.

'Far off is my home,' she said. 'Far and far.' She turned impulsively towards them. 'I thank you, Torr and Tara, and you, too, Frelgar .I owe you more than a life, more than my own comfort and freedom from torture. For I owe you the life of my unborn golden egg, that I would never have laid for Zirmazd the Cruel had he chained me for ten thousand years.'

The blood thumped in Torr's veins as he looked on her.

'We stand awed before your beauty,' he said, huskily, and foolishly conscious of the bumpkin-like gallantry of the remark. But – that was how he felt, and he was not ashamed of the feeling.

She laughed.

Ishrivara the Golden laughed.

'I have not laughed for long and long – and, Torr Vorkun of Darkholm – had you golden feathers or had I a naked skin – I could have loved you, loved you dearly!'

'And I – you!'

'Now I see you ride north westwards – and I must fly north-eastwards – or thereabouts. And I mislike flying within the confines of a forest. So – '

'So it is goodbye, Ishrivara,' said Tara, simply.

With a great golden fluttering Ishrivara from the back of her dryne rose into the air. She turned then, there in the bright sunshot air, twisting and diving, turning and rolling, joying as no earthbound mortal could comprehend in the glory of flight.

Swayingly, she fluttered before Frelgar and took his hand. Hovering, she kissed Tara with warm sisterly affection.

Then – then she clung for a moment to Torr Vorkun, kissing him so that the blood firmed in him, kising him with all of farewell love and passion.

With a flashing glint of wings she rose.

Her voice carolled down.

'Farewell, good friends. My undying thanks to you – and so now, goodbye!'

They watched her, unspeaking, they watched as those golden pinions strong beating carried her away until she dwindled smaller and smaller until at last only a single golden gleam flashed out – then she was gone.

'I – liked her!' said Tara Vorkun.

'She had a gaiety of spirit that all the caging in the world could not break,' said Frelgar.

But Torr Vorkun of Darkholm in Drugay said nothing.

Only – only he touched, gently, his lips where her golden lips had rested.

For the rest of that day they rode hard but in a subdued silence. They husbanded the strengths of the drynes as best they could, riding turn and turn about, with four mounts to press into service by rota. They stopped once, in a tiny glade by a tree-bowered stream, to drink and to fill their ravenous stomachs with the dried meats and fruits packed in their saddlebags. The drynes cropped the grass, quietly.

'Good animals,' commented Frelgar as they mounted up again.

The beasts indeed must have been the pick of the stables. Their eagle-like heads and beaks, strapped now in brass-riveted red velvet did not try to champ and open against the restraints. Their bird-like bodies, yellow-feathered with a few opalescent blue and green feathers where the rudimentary tail joined the plump body, moved with a swaying side to side rhythm on their two stem-like bird legs. Their stub wings, barely nine inches long, lay beneath their saddle-coverings to give a wider and more comfortable support. That those cruel eagle-beaked jaws could clip grass – with a funny sideways dipping movement of the whole bird neck – spoke eloquently of much long and arduous training. For the dryne habitually fed on flesh.

'Zirmazd kept his word,' commented Torr dryly.

They made camp that night with the rugs and clothes rolled in their saddlebags. Torr set no watch. He had a growing confidence in Frelgar's self-abnegation of thaumaturgical powers. Somehow, he understood, that very rejection of sorcery conferred protection on the Pragmatist against wizardry. And some of that protection spilled over on to his companions. Resting with a heart nearer peacefulness than at any time since they had entered this land of Gamelon with its remote king and his Prefects to carry out his commands, Torr thought back to his own last lord, the Lord High King of the League of Praterxes. Now – there *had* been a king! He guessed that the imminent invasion of the new people from what was called Garthland had given the king of all the Land of Gamelon and his Prefects bad dreams of nights. He did not know how much further beyond this forest the writ of Gamelon ran, or how much further westwards beyond that they would meet the new people. He hoped it was not as far as the distance they had come from the south-east.

To the north-west the Opal Sea washed all these shores with a mysterious promise of far horizons, and to the north-east the main bulk of the Land of Gamelon, protected here by the March of Gamelon, extended he did not know for how far. He thought of Ishrivara of the golden feathers, and sighed.

Tomorrow, they would march again westwards. Until they reached the end of this land, until they met the barring strands of some mighty sea, westwards he would go until they either failed, or found Jaran the All-seeing. As for Frelgar, he well understood how that man cared not where he went so long as he could practice his Pragmatism.

Frelgar was a handy blade to have along.

He slept, then, deeply and peacefully.

In the morning they saddled up and set off. Frelgar began to sing the interminable verses of some low song. Tara made no comment and, to Torr's secret but unexpressed disappointment, did not join in. He always loved the gay careless singing of Tara of the silver voice.

'You ate sparingly this morning,' he said, casually.

'Aye,' she said shortly. And then, a little breathlessly : 'This Amadis-forsaken Black Bodice is tight on me today.'

The Black Bodice encinctured her body without seam or join and all their attempts to cut the strange material had resulted only in chafing Tara's flesh. Now Torr swung to Frelgar.

'Frelgar, friend, cannot you spell one small enchantment and free Tara of this monstrous incumbrance?'

Frelgar stopped singing and shook his head.

'For the sake of our new-found and precious comradeship?'

'I have forsworn all sorcery.'

'But – but even for good ends, Frelgar?'

'For any ends. I preach the essential dignity of mankind.'

And so that remained that, it would seem. They rode on, all that day and the next, and on the following day they rode out of the Forest of Greater Stretting and entered on to an endless undulating plain, dotted with thrifty trees and water courses and where herds of hoofed animals reared their heads and tossed their manes and raced with the thunder of Valkur and his warriors from the approach of the humans.

Avoiding the occasional hamlet secluded where a road crossed a river they pressed on. Tara wheezed. She rode half hitched up in her saddle, as though sitting a red-hot needle. Torr, perplexed and anxious, reined in.

'Tara – for the sweet sake of Precious Amadis herself – tell me what is wrong ! '

She showed him a pinched face.

'The Black Bodice – I had not wanted to alarm you. I reck well we must put as many leagues as we can between us and the vengeance of Lohr Prendil. And yet – and yet I can scarce ride

68

more – '

'Tara!'

Frelgar turned his head away.

Stonily, he said : 'I told you I had heard of the Black Bodice.
I – Oh, for the sweet humanity of man to man! That I could –
that I have sworn by everything sacred that I will not – oh, Torr,
Tara, pity me now!'

'Pity you!' shouted Torr, his nostrils tight, his eyes glaring
with sudden understanding. He half drew Lycheaper. 'What of
Tara? What of my sister?'

'The Black Bodice,' said Frelgar numbly. 'It grows smaller.
It is part of its demon-driven power. It will shrink, tighter and
tighter, cutting and constricting – '

Tara moaned.

'It'll cut her in half!' yelled Torr. 'It will crush her to – '

'There is nothing we can do!' cried Frelgar in the agony of
his spirit.

'Nothing!' screamed Torr Vorkun of Darkholm. 'Must I sit
and watch my sister crushed to a bloody death?'

'Aye – you must!'

Hippogryph: half horse, half griffin--a
snarling monster from the dim netherworld.

A Dragonel, the Medieval name for a young dragon not yet arrived at total maturity.

This ray-like creature is from the "Book
of Grotesques." It could fly, walk, swim.

An illustration from the ghoulish "Book of
Grotesques," celebrated history of monsters.

The Manticore monster of ancient Tatary, a
territory where hideous creatures lurked.

Pig-headed devil monster. One of the most
feared, most ferocious of all grotesques.

The dragon Diabolus, a hideous brute which
stalked the dark recesses of fantasy world.

166

Throughout Eastern fantasy this frightful
thing haunts the minds of ordinary mortals.

Two Fighting Manicoras locked in a deadly
battle for control of their fantasy world.

The Flying Serpent is a fantasy grotesque familiar to all the cultures of the world.

816   817   818

819   820

A gallery of some of the weirdest creatures
ever dreamed up by the feverish mind of man.

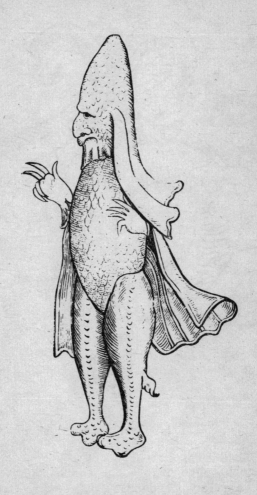

This hideous thing was first "seen" in the
Black Forest and may still be lurking there.

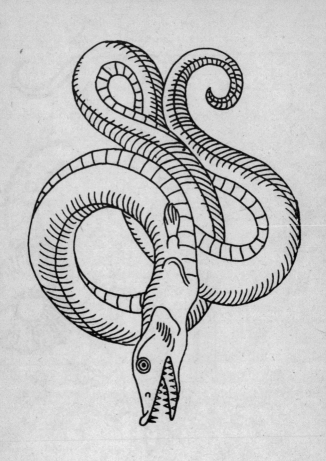

Sea serpent of the Middle Ages. It bears
some resemblance to the Loch Ness Monster.

Basilisk, or Cocatrice, the dreadful bird
monster described in German fantasy tales.

In the world of fantasy, monsters no less awful than those on land lurk in the sea.

More fabulous creatures from the "Book of
Grotesques," published in the Middle Ages.

8

Teryxes from Sjombalku

In a grassy dell beside a merry stream beneath the overhanging branches of a jonran stand of young trees, Torr stared in agony at his sister's agony.

Her waist had been cohstricted in cruelly. Torr wrenched away the concealing cloak. He gasped.

'That this should be!' he said, brokenly.

Tara's waist spanned less than his two spread hands. Her breasts bulged proud-standing above and her hips jutted, their bones prominent and shining, below. He could not get the point of Lycheaper between her flesh and the blasphemous black material of the bodice. She winced but did not cry out as the sharp blade nicked her.

'Only a superior necromancy,' he said, holding on to the panic that threatened to topple his reason. He could understand the death of his sister in battle, even in childbed; but this – this slow remorseless obscenity of death, crushed, splintering and broken and bloody, between the constricting hands of black sorcery – this, he could not face. 'A superior thaumaturgical lore,' he said again, his jaws aching, his eyes sore. 'Very well, if that is how it must be, that is how it will be!'

'What do you mean?'

'Follow me. And, Tara, my beloved sister, do you ride with us and bear your pain as a Drugayan may who has known the meaning of suffering.'

'Yes, my brother.' She did not say more. Breathing hurt.

He urged the drynes into savage motion, kicking his feet into the yellow feathered bodies, thwacking the flat of his sword across the other's tails. Kicking dust, they sped across that endless plain.

'Quapartz – well-named the Bloody-handed! If ever you and I meet again, spells or no, your head flies from your shoulders!'

They rode on. Tara's face showed the agony she suffered; yet she kept her silence within herself, holding on to her courage with fragile yet unbreakable resolution.

Towards evening in this mad ride it seemed to nowhere they swung aside to let a file of Gamelon soldiery past. They rode drynes with dark blood still spattering their feathers. Two men in their bronze link mail over the puce tunics lolled in the saddles, and the bright blood coughed from their mouths and ran down over their chins. Gashes, bloody and smoking, had been rent in their mail. The soldiers carried their lances all crooked, their heads hanging, and the air of defeat stamped over them brought grim satisfaction to Torr Vorkun.

The three travellers let the soldiers past until the shadows of evening swallowed them. Then they pressed on. Torr would not rest. He asked Tara if she could continue, and received a tight nod in reply. He did not question Frelgar. That man – that Pragmatist – might keep up if he wished or not. All Torr's hopes lay ahead of them.

Towards the morning when the chill wind of dawn brushed their cloaks and the stars began to dance their twinkling way back into Father Uran's ebon chest to make way for His fiery chariot, Tara toppled from the saddle.

Torr jumped to her, lifted her head. She tried to smile at him, wrenching his spirit with the agony of the moment. Frelgar reined and waited, still and grim and unspeaking.

Torr lifted his head, pleading, suffering, begging.

'Frelgar – Frelgar, will you not lift this curse from my sister? Please – I beg you, on my knees – '

'I cannot, Torr, I am forsworn . . .

Like a maniac then, Torr Vorkun sprang up. He dragged out Lycheaper, leaped on the Pragmatist, knocked him from the saddle. Panting like a beast of the jungle Torr Vorkun stood straddle-legged over the blocky body of Frelgar, put the point of his sword against the ridged throat, pushed.

'So help me, Frelgar! If you do not use your powers to remove this Black Bodice I thrust home!'

Frelgar closed his eyes. 'Thrust home, then, Torr Vorkun!

Gasping, red-eyed, his muscles trembling uncontrollably, Torr Vorkun leaned down on his sword.

'Break the black enchantment, Frelgar! You who prate of man's humanity to man! Use your arts – the arts of thaumaturgical lore you learned as a child and a grown man, practicing wizardry! Release my sister – *or you die*!'

'Then I must die, Torr. It has been a bright time with you – full of unexpected twists of fortune – but I must retain my trust. I cannot break my own faith! Even for you – even for a man I would count a true friend. Strike, Torr Vorkun of whatsit – strike home!'

The low, suffering cry reached Torr through the mad wash of blood dinning in his ears.

'No, Torr! No! Let him live – I respect his – his . . . '

But Tara Vorkun could not go on. She sagged back, her face congested, her eyes closed, her body shaped to a blasphemous parody of those hour glasses used aboard the carracks of the Opal Sea.

'Tara! Tara my beloved sister!'

Torr threw Lycheaper from him. He tossed the bright blade spinning in the cold morning light. He lowered his head into his hands and crouched, a ball of misery, beaten, thrashed like a cur dog of the gutters of Gamelon Town.

'Torr –' Weakly she called.

He crawled to her, held her hand, smoothed her hair, kissed her cheek. He could not bear to look on her twisted body. He felt the grip of her fingers, constricting in desolate imitation of the Black Bodice constricting about her slender waist.

He heard a thunder of beating wings and dark shadows slanted athwart the low-rising sun and for a moment he thought that Ishrivara, the golden flying girl, had returned. Then he looked up and saw –

And saw giant winged beasts all ashimmer in the morning sun descending towards him with men perched on their backs, men of wild aspect and flowing black hair and harsh brutal faces, wielding long lances and brandishing double-handed swords. They landed about him in a cascading fluttering. Metal clanged. Harsh voices challenged. Lance tips prodded at his body ungently. In words that he could barely comprehend so outlandish were the accents he heard these outriders from the new people speaking to him.

'Up, stranger! Let us look on you!'

A voice of authority, deep-bass and strong. 'Their hair! See their hair, comrades!'

Dully Torr stood up. He realised these must be the scouts who had beaten the Gamelon cavalry they had seen the previous evening. Tough men, flying their strange beasts through the air, they must have overwhelmed the Gamelon puce and bronze without mercy, leaving only a remnant to escape.

These men wore flying leathers of brilliant shining green, studded with bronze, with black boots to their knees and with low-crowned leather and bronze helmets with tall crests of multi-hued feathers waving in the sunshine. Their faces were broad, strong, with high cheekbones and glittering black eyes. Their lips gashed their bronzed faces. And their hair – their hair! Black and luxurious and flowing, it cascaded from beneath their helmets in defiant profusion, a direct and unequivocal challenge to the red of Gamelon.

'What ails the girl?' demanded the leader, a scarred warrior who wore a scarlet sash about his bulky waist.

Torr Vorkun roused himself. He remembered who he was and he remembered his planned determination, and some of his old steely purpose returned.

'We are foes to all of Gamelon!' he shouted. He tried to twist his tongue into the wider vowel-sounds of these men, to make them understand without possibility of mistake. Where language had originated no man knew; but men could talk to men throughout the length and breadth of the land. 'We fought our way clear of Gamelon to join you – but the wizard Quarpartz the Bloody-handed left this vile contraption about my sister. I ask you, of your mercy and your wisdom, take me to your sorcerer-in-chief. Let him remove this devilish enchantment!'

'Softly, softly, lad,' growled the leader. 'Not so fast.'

'Speed is vital!' Pushing aside the lance points Torr leaped up. 'Only a superior necromancy can remove this Black Bodice – and I thought to find that with you people. But if you think your wizards unable to mend the mischief of the wizards of Gamelon –' He let it hang.

A young buck with a profusion of blue and cerise feathers sprouting from his helmet guffawed.

'They are peasants, Kar Sjontu! Mere oafs! Spies for Gamelon. Let us kill the men and make sport with the girl before she is cut in half!'

'Silence, Wolfsbane! I am in command—'

Torr Vorkun took the opportunity as a slipping climber seizes a rock among the snows of the peaks.

'Let Wolfsbane fight me, and he will. He will find me harder to kill than a wolf. I fight for my sister's honour and for your promise—'

Kar Sjontu interrupted. A glancing smile touched his craggy lips. 'Enough! I make no promises that a knight may not keep. If you can keep Wolfsbane from killing you then we will take you back. That seems a chivalrous thing to do, eh comrades?'

The others roared their approval. Torr began to understand a little of their ethos then.

Wolfsbane dismounted arrogantly. A strong, tall youth, with his black hair flowing, his green leather armour glittering in the early sunshine, he selected a long straight sword of steel from the armoury at his saddle bow.

'An axeman, I see,' he nodded at Murgur's great axe thonged to Torr's dryne's saddle. 'My sword will have little difficulty with you, peasant. And your sister—'

If the arrogant youngster expected that to enrage Torr so that he would rush in with all a naïve barbarian's anger, he mistook his man. Mention of Tara gave Torr that extra icy grip on his resolve. He took down Murgur's axe. Lycheaper lay where it had fallen, among the grasses.

He unhitched the quiver and laid it aside. He shrugged off the midnight-blue cloak. The bow, unstrung, he had kept strapped to the dryne's saddle for ease of riding.

Wolfsbane strutted forward cockily. A good swordsman, evidently, by his grip and stance, he anticipated handling this axeman as any swordsman would – as Torr had done.

The shrieking pressure on him to hurry! hurry! hurry! clamoured in Torr. He hefted Murgur's black-thonged axe. He slanted it up over his left shoulder. Wolfsbane danced in.

The axe swept down, the black-haired man glided sideways

and his blade snaked out to score down Torr's side. The axe cut back and only Wolfsbane's wild leap saved him. A fixed grin extended his lips. His eyes took on a transparent stare. Again he slashed short, reversed, tried to hew through Torr's thigh. Torr sliped the blow; but his answering axe-stroke hissed through empty air.

This would take too long.

Holding his raging anger in he shortened his grip on the axe, held it as he would a spear or a halberd, jumped to his left. Wolfsbane turned with him, the sword a bar of steel in the sunshine. With all the speed no ordinary man could hope to counter, Torr smashed to his right, thrust in and down, aiming for the thigh, pierced his man through, released his left hand grip and caught Wolfsbane's sword arm in a grip that constricted – constricted! – twisted, ground bones, forced the rigid hand open wide so that the sword fell to the grass.

With one foot on the sword, Torr stood over the fallen man. He jerked the axe free and cocked it. The blades cut cruel patterns against the sky.

'Now, Wolfsbane, do you cry mercy or do I sever your head from your body?'

Grimly, unyielding, Kar Sjontu leaned on his saddle bow, silent, watchful.

With maniac hatred Wolfsbane glared up. He read death in the brown eyes of Torr Vorkun.

'I yield,' he gasped, grudgingly. 'I cry you mercy.'

Torr stepped away. He could allow himself no feelings of relief, of reaction. He turned to Kar Sjontu.

'Was it fair fight?'

'Aye. As fair as I've seen – mayhap the play lent itself to a hand grip – the marshals would have to rule on that. I am but a hard fighting man myself, with little relish for the new chivalry that demands un-manning rules.'

'My sister is in sore need – '

'Your weird bird-beasts will be useless. They could never keep up with out teryxes. They fly faster than the swallows in spring.'

A sound brought Torr about. Tara Vorkun was laboriously dragging herself across the grass, her face fixed in a set resolve.

She reached the crouched form of Wolfsbane. From his pierced thigh the bright arterial blood pumped. He would be dead within the hour. She bent over him, her tortured body twisted. Her hands moved. Wolfsbane jerked away, then groaned with pain and remained still. Moments later Tara tried to leave, moaned, collapsed sideways into Torr's ready arms.

'I could not – ' she whispered. 'I can still work my healing magic, as ever – as ever – he should not die – '

Wolfsbane's hideous wound had closed up and no blood showed.

Grimly, Kar Sjontu nodded. 'I recognise chivalry when I see it, even if these pampered dandies of today have other ideas.' He roared an order. 'Sjri, Sjallu, do you stay with Wolfsbane. Give up your mounts to these strangers. They have need of them. Our patrol is done and we have the news we came for. If this girl is to be saved she must reach Shishu-Sji before this night is out. Follow on those bird monstrosities – we had sport with such as them yester even!'

'Aye!' roared his men, relishing the memory of combat.

Torr walked across the grass and retrieved Lycheaper, slipping the trusty blade into the old dragobrane scabbard. They helped Tara mount up, solicitous with her, padding her body with rugs, strapping her into the saddle with sure fingers. He paused by Frelgar as that Pragmatist wriggled about on the teryx, settling his feet into the embroidered and silver-mounted stirrups.

'Frelgar – new friend but old friend in feeling – I am – I am – '

'Don't say you are sorry, Torr. I think I would have done the same. It is I who should be sorry for the sins of the world that bring man and man to threats of killing. All I pray is that you try to understand that I will not break my vow – I cannot – for now I am a Pragmatist!' Sweat stood on Frelgar's forehead, and his eyes showed inner pain.

Torr swung away without another word and mounted up. He found the seat comfortable, well padded and with many straps and embroidered ropes to make sure he would not fall off. In a great clashing of wings the flying beasts rose into the air, leaving the unflying birds below.

In a bunch they headed out, away from the rising sun, heading due westwards.

Torr Vorkun vowed then that he would take Tara his sister to Shishu-Sji through oceans of blood if need be and force the wizard no matter what the cost to free the Black Bodice.

9

The Higher Sorcery of Shishu-Sji

All that day they flew with the untiring beat of teryx pinions hurling them on ever westwards. The fanged jaws and wedge-shaped head of the teryx Torr rode held high before him, the long neck upcurving like that of a swan, so that he could recline on the streamlined body and receive some protection from the blustering windflow. Spanning over thirty feet, the powerful wings beat with a rhythmic swaying motion that lulled. The teryx kept its scarlet-clawed feet tucked up beneath its dove-like tail, its green and blue feathers sheening in the sun with a matching brilliance to the green bronze-studded flying leathers of the new people. They called themselves the flower of chivalry, the knights of the air, the outriders to the hosts of Sjombalku. They possessed the fascination of all things new to Torr of Darkholm and he felt a restless surge of anticipation drive him on. Surely, now, he would find the sorcerer who could strike off the Black Bodice from the fair form of his sister Tara!

As the afternoon waned and a rumble from his belly told him that as ever he needed food he tossed aside that minor pre-occupation. He could not stop for eating and self-gluttony whilst his sister suffered – by the disgusting swag belly of Obese Rumphaldi Himself – no!

In the gathering shadows below as they flew now directly into the sinking orb of the sun he could see long trains of marching people, hosts of mounted men riding beasts he could not identify, seemingly unending columns of covered wagons surrounded by a horde of walking women and children. Fires began to dot the plain with scraps of light, fighting the shadows. Other teryxes swung in on wimpling wings against the sunset to land in vast conclaves of wing-beating, shrilling, dusty huddlings for the night.

They headed for a cluster of tents, the lights within shining bravely through the canvas and the cloths, indifferent to the night animals and all potential foes. The new people, the hosts of Sjombalku, marched eastwards with sure confidence in their own fighting strengths.

The teryxes landed and Torr as once, his straps already unbuckled, leaped down without caring for the stiffness the long flight had brought to his sinews. He reached Tara. She lay held by her straps and bindings, unconscious, her face blue and frighteningly cold.

He ripped the bindings away and lifted her down, tenderly.

'Take me to Shishu-Sji at once, Kar Sjontu!' he shouted.

'Wait, wait, lad. He must be apprised – he may not be available immediately –'

Torr Vorkun had not ridden so stubbornly westwards with his sister in agony without a plan. He had known he would meet the new people sooner or later, and sooner by all the omens. Now he spoke out the plan he had formed.

'He will see us, by Valkur! And now! Tell him I am come from Gamelon Town and I have news – news that he will hear when my sister is free from the Black Bodice.'

'Tzorisj! You did not tell me you had information!'

'Aye! And if my sister dies white hot brands will not tear it from me!'

'I believe you,' said Kar Sjontu, darkly. He strode away and Torr, carrying Tara cradled in his arms, followed. He heard the faithful footsteps of Frelgar paddling in the rear.

At the entrance to a tent that stood out from the others by reason of its midnight black and the stars and moons patterned upon it, Kar Sjontu halted and spoke to a guard who stood blockily before the tent flap. As large as a house of Gamelon Town, the tent showed many peaks and ridges, many guy ropes, many black flags vague against the night sky. Lights glowed within. But Torr glared at the guard.

Not a man – that was his first impression. A being, a being with thick-muscled arms – four of them – and wearing on his black-haired body a kilt of red bronze links, and a corselet of bronze plates, linked by mail, and mail sleeves over those four arms that held a falchion and a shield. But the face! The face glared wired-whiskery like that of a rat, sharp-nosed, razor-toothed, spike-eyed. Its pink ears shone translucently from the light from the tent. Now it growled gutturally in its throat and the broad falchion switched up.

'It is Kar Sjontu – with urgent business for Shishu-Sji. Announce us immediately!'

But the rat-faced being growled a guttural and swung the falchion offensively, waving Kar Sjontu away. Once more the patrol leader asked for admittance. But the guard would have none of it. Frustrated, Kar Sjontu swung about.

'The wizard is performing sacred rites – he cannot be disturbed for three hours yet – and then he may decide to sleep – '

But Torr Vorkun stopped listening. He thrust Tara's tight-cased body at Frelgar and that man's brawny arms grasped her with a strange tenderness. Torr strode directly to the beast-man guard.

'Let me in! For I am Torr Vorkun of Darkholm of Drugay and I have news for Shishu-Sji! At once!'

The only answer, an immediate one, was a blow from the flat of the falchion. With his own beast-instincts, Torr rode the blow. But the steel smacked stunningly into his cheek, staggering him. He shook his head.

'Nothing is stopping me now!'

Lycheaper flamed.

The falchion clanged once, twice, then Lycheaper flicked past the upthrust shield and twisted, and the falchion span through the air. A maddened barbarian would have thrust to kill, then. But Torr Vorkun recked where he was and of the hosts of Sjombalku around him in the breathing night, and of the cost of an unnecessary death to his cause now. He turned his wrist over and laid the flat of Lycheaper alongside the beast-man's rat-like head. The guard tumbled.

With Lycheaper naked in his hand Torr Vorkun strode into the wizard's tent. Bearing Tara in his arms, Frelgar followed.

A charnel house stench stank in his nostrils.

Between the supporting posts of the many-peaked tent he saw the familiar paraphernalia of a necromancer's lair. The wired skeleton did not look completely human. A row of skulls along a shelf, the blasphemous milky falsity of the root of the wombscrawn tree, a whole cupboard full of vials and containers of magical powders and devilish liquids, all told him that this magician wielded powers that should serve his ends.

Beyond the first partition formed of hanging Shandascrine rugs, looted from a noble's house, no doubt, a pentacle had been formed in the heavier rugs of the floor, native Sjombalku rugs depicting obscene rites and unmentionable creatures. Within the pentacle a whiff of smoke dissipated. A form writhed there, fading and disappearing, thinning, vanishing as Torr's quick eyes adjusted. He breathed out the charnel stink with an oath.

Shishu-Sji moved to face him from the far side of the pentacle.

'I am glad, outlander, that you did not kill my Dentro guard. They are loyal if stupid creatures.'

Torr's muscles jumped.

'If you knew – as I imagine you must have known if your thaumaturgical powers are as great as I have been led to believe – why did you have him stop me? You know I wish you no harm. I crave your help – '

'That I know. But I was in converse with my familiar, Sjik, and you know – '

'Have done, sorcerer! I ask a boon – strike from my sister this accursed Black Bodice – and my aid is yours! '

Shishu-Sji moved mincingly from the pentacle smoke, stood thoughtfully before Torr. He seemed a shrunken little man, with a flat cap of magical runes, a long robe without adornment save for a single star high on his left shoulder. All of scarlet, that robe, with the golden star shining in the lights of the braziers, all of a scarlet that brought tears to the eyes.

'And what does the Lord of the Earth and of Thunder say to this your request?'

'Who?'

Breathing a trifle unsteadily, Kar Sjontu had entered this wizard's den. 'The Lord of the Earth and of Thunder, Torr Vorkun. Our liege lord here on this earth! The only true commander of the Hosts of Sjombalku! '

'There is no time!' snapped Torr. 'See, my sister – the Black Bodice is cutting her in two! She cannot live much longer – her ribs will snap – her flesh will crush –'

Shishu-Sji peered. His shrunken cheeks with their stubble of white, and his stringy white beard stained with brown, and his faded eyes made him look old and doddering. But Torr was not deceived. Here was a sorcerer far removed from poor Zirmazd the Wily, far more to be feared, even, than Quapartz the Bloody-handed.

'I know of the Black Bodice –' he began.

'Save me the market-place clapman's spiel!' raged Torr. 'I know you know – and I know you can free my sister. What is required to be done, that will I do!'

'Ah, so?'

'Ah, so! Now, Wizard, will you, for the sweet sake of Amadis herself, get on with it!'

'Bring no false gods here!' warned Kar Sjontu, uneasily.

Over against the hanging rugs a couch stood, with clawed feet and inscribed lintels. Here Frelgar, without speaking, placed Tara. He arranged her arms along her sides. They touched her upper side, and then her hips. The curved space between shrieked its silent menace. Torr raged at Shishu-Sji.

'Hurry, magician! Perform your thaumaturgical arts! Remove that horror.– now!'

Frelgar had gone across to a shelf and now returned bearing three bottles, one indigo, one amber, one emerald. These he placed on the floor beside Tara. Then he picked up a golden knife from a shrine beside a tent pole where incense coiled. This knife, hilt first, he handed to Shishu-Sji. The necromancer looked at Frelgar as though Sintian's Gates had burst.

'Who – who are you, stranger?'

'I will tell you when you have performed the rite of ossification and of sundering. Hurry!'

The wizard shook his head. 'I cannot plumb you –'

Without recking now, now that he was so close, Torr drew Lycheaper from the scabbard where he had sheathed it after entering here. He half lifted the brand.

'Now, by all the greater gods and all the lesser godlings of all the countries in the world! Strike me down now, Shishu-

Sji, whilst you have the chance! For if you do not free my sister this minute I run my blade through your heart!'

Shishu-Sji waved him away with a hand of surprising plumpness, and the many talismanic rings with their sigils of power flamed in the brazier and torch light. He inclined his head.

'I could strike you now, outlander – but – but you are rude and uncouth and understand nothing.' He took the golden knife Frelgar held out. 'But this man – this man is the one!'

Frelgar stood aside, and his sly smile curved those firm lips as much as to say that this wizard, too, was but a mortal man.

The magician bent to the bottles. Into each one in turn he plunged the knife, turning the coloured liquid to an inner golden glow. He muttered words that meant nothing to Torr and yet which contained the power to breeze an icy chill along the nape of his neck. Through that chill he felt a furnace blast radiate from the knife that brought sweat to his forehead and armpits and concaved the hollowness of his belly.

Now the knife glowed!

It shone resplendent, drowning torch light in a radiating glory.

Torr caught the word 'ossification'. The knife waved strange symbolings in the smoky air.

High, in both hands, high and tautly Shishu-Sji held the knife. The point hung above the cleavage between Tara's breasts, directly over the beginning of that binding black sheath that would turn into a midnight winding shroud.

Torr tensed. If the wizard played him false now – He'd smash Lycheaper through that traitorous heart even if only a worm-shape drove the blade!

Down descended the glowing golden knife. Closer and closer to that strange greenish-black-rust hued material. Smarting tears sprang stinging into Torr's eyes; but he brushed them away. He would not turn his gaze aside now.

The point kissed the hem of the Black Bodice. Like treacle beneath a heated knife the material shrivelled. It shrank back from that slicing point. Down between Tara's breasts, over the constricted well of her stomach, directly over her navel, down and down to the bottom hem of the girdle, the golden knife moved in the plump hands of Shishu-Sji.

And the Black Bodice fell asunder!

Torr stared appalled at the shark-belly whiteness of his sister's skin. Slowly, slowly, the red blood began to creep back. Her stomach moved, jerkily. A low moan of pain escaped past her lips.

'Quick, fumbler!' roared Frelgar. 'A potion of sleep for the girl! Let her recover in the bliss of sleep!'

Quickly, Shishu-Sji poured a foaming crimson drink into a beaker, and between them they lifted Tara's head and made her drink. She slumped back, shrivelled, white, a sight that brought back all Torr's fears for his sister.

'She looks – ' he said, throatily. 'She – will she?'

'She will sleep and recover now, Torr,' said Frelgar. The Pragmatist stepped back, and took a deep breath. 'I came very close to breaking my vows, then, through friendship.'

'Thank you, Frelgar,' said Torr, simply.

'She will need a long rest.' Shishu-Sji spoke with some force in an attempt to regain the superiority in matters thaumaturgical he considered his right. 'I will have my handmaidens see she is cared for.' He stared at Torr. 'You may trust me. I have promised nothing, and by that token is my trust assured.' He rang a small silver bell and at once half-naked sprites in white gossamer appeared and cooed over Tara, began to wash her travel-stained body and to rub soothing ointments into her bruised flesh. Torr hesitated.

'Come away, man!' snapped the wizard. 'Sit and eat and refresh yourself.'

Reluctantly, yet seeing that he had now no other discourse, Torr obeyed. They sat at an octagonal table where meats and fruits and flat dough-cakes lay spread on silver plates and where flagons of cool ale waited their attention.

'You can wash afterwards, outlander. Now – tell me your news!'

Torr Vorkun chuckled.

What news had he? He had lied – he recked nothing of any lie, any act, that would save his sister. But now he must lie again, and with cool cunning, against all the arts of a master wizard.

10

The Challenge

'I would wash myself now, before I eat,' he said, firmly. 'And, Shishu-Sji – I would thank you, sincerely, for removing that black blasphemy from my sister.'

The old sorcerer waved that away. 'Thank me not for an act of mercy. I have performed many black arts in my time – Tzorisj knows – and yet dearer to me by far are the healing arts, and the magic of maintenance whereby are our great Hosts of Sjombalku made great and puissant in the land.'

'But I am a foreigner –'

'As to that, a man is a man.' Shishu-Sji glanced at Frelgar at that moment, a bird-like craning of the neck.

Frelgar smiled his wry smile.

'Yes, Shishu-Sji. I am a Pragmatist –'

The wizard waved that aside. 'As I had surmised – for you know no wizard can riddle a Pragmatist –'

Frelgar smiled again.

Washing himself thoroughly, Torr listened, and thought shrewdly on the ways and means to his hand. His calculating mind weighed the wizard's shrewdness for, despite all his magic lore, the necromancer could not be absolutely sure, could not know for certain, that Torr Vorkun lied. The eagerness in the wizard betokened a thirst for knowledge out of Gamelon that paralleled the hunger for news out of Garthland of the Prefect. There was profit to be made of that. He shaved himself with the edge of Lycheaper, clean and smooth, thinking back to the last time he had done this, in the greenwood with Tara and Frelgar – oh, it seemed, ages agone.

'Now, outlander, come and drink and fill your belly with good country fare. For we of the Sjombalku feast well!'

A smooth man, this wizard, and yet, and yet, was he smooth,

or was he naturally generous and kind? A sorcerer? Torr thought of Frelgar, and wondered anew at the vagaries of men.

Eating and drinking, he said between mouthfuls: 'What is the one thing you wish to know above all else about Gamelon Town?'

The wizard leaned forward. 'I have tried to penetrate their wizards' spells; but they are strong. I can see a great deal; but always the final seeing is misty, indistinct. The information the Lord of the Earth and of Thunder would have is not so much strictly military as of moral value. Their morale. Their spirit for the coming fight. Their trust in their wizards – '

'As to the latter, they have no choice.'

'I see.' Shishu-Sji sipped ruby wine from a goblet of crystal. They lived high, these new people, their arts and their crafts of a standard that would not have shamed the palaces and tables of the Lord High King. 'I clash in the spirit world with a black necromancer called Quapartz – '

'Him!' said Torr Vorkun. 'Him I will flay and roast on his own griddle!'

'Many a time has he dealt me a sore buffet. Perhaps you have news of a weakness – ?'

'Only that if I can get Lycheaper to his throat before he turns me into a frog I'll settle his business for him.'

'We have sent spies into Gamelon Town; but they are caught. Our young men refuse to cut their black hair; and all the dyes in the world cannot long subdue their natural colour.'

'I saw a couple, strung up, their guts hanging out,' put in Frelgar.

Kar Sjontu, who had been invited to the table, rasped an oath. 'By Ztasjofree! They will be avenged!'

The necromancer leaned closer. 'Your news, outlander?'

Torr Vorkun took a breath. 'You can strike at Gamelon Town through the wizard Zirmazd the Wily. He is old, a dodderer, a fumbler, frightened for his life, unable to riddle you new people, ripe meat for pressure!'

Shishu-Sji looked his surprise. His white brows drew together.

'Of him I have not heard.'

It was Torr's turn to be surprised.

'You have battled on the astral plane with Quapartz the Bloody-handed; yet you have not encountered Zirmazd the Wily. That is passing strange.'

Frelgar took on a vacant look, quaffing rich ruby wine, crumbling a doughy cake with his strong fingers.

'What of Gamelon March?' put in Kar Sjontu. 'And of all the Land of Gamelon beyond?'

'We came up from the south-east, and then struck westwards seeking you. All the lands out to the east and north east, where lies the chief strength of Gamelon, are unknown to us. I have heard of the countries of Naulochus, and of Erendapalla and Cremna and of the wondrous cities of Esdraphon and of Taxella-without-Walls – if such an unbelievable thing as a city without walls can be – and once, in a cave in the Quorum Hills far from here, of the fabled land of Sog-wher-Pyrgi where men are said to have an eye in their chests and to walk on their hands. But –'

'Spare me this recital of travellers' tales, fit only for children around the camp fire! Gamelon Town!'

'Stay –' said Shishu-Sji. 'The south east?'

'Khurdisrane, Vorkandalung, Blessed Paltomir, capital of the League of Praterxes –'

The wizard shook his head. 'Perhaps you had better tell us what you know of Gamelon Town itself.' He rubbed a plump sigil-encrusted finger down his nose. 'This Zirmazd must be explored. He must be a lever. This is interesting news you bring, if disturbing.'

Torr let his breath out. He picked up a goblet and drank with the feeling of relief strong on him. Then he told the men of Sjombalku all that he knew of Gamelon Town, information that Frelgar was able to amplify.

When they had done Kar Sjontu rumbled a pleased oath. 'From the way that weird bird-mounted cavalry patrol fought when we jumped them, I'd say the people of Gamelon have no stomach for the fight! We will roll up. And then, perhaps, our long march may cease and we can find a new home.'

Torr Vorkun thought of the horrors beneath the castle of Gamelon Town. 'You would needs clean the place up.'

'Aye! We would burn out the foul vipers' nests and have done!'

'Kar, Kar!' protested Shishu-Sji, half laughing. 'Leave us one stone upon another to start with!'

'Maybe, and maybe not,' said Kar Sjontu, grimly.

A slight commotion at the door heralded the Dentro guard whose rat-like eyes surveyed Torr without emotion.

He gobbled his gowly tongue at Kar Sjontu. That tough warrior arose, apologising.

'It is Kar Sjastry and Kar Sjoylem. We have a rendezvous tonight with certain ladies of – well, never mind that. They are good knightly drinking companions, never fear.' He winked.

When he had gone, Torr said : 'Kar? What of Kar?'

Shishu-Sji sipped his wine. 'A title, a title conferred on a knight after he has performed a doughty deed. When he wins his spurs, he becomes a knight high Kar.'

Torr nodded, understanding. This chivalry might be different from that of the League of Praterxes, in which Torr had early won his own spurs as a knight, and certainly it was vastly different from the rough near-barbarism of far Drugay's code of warfare; but he would no doubt easily learn the further ramifications if he stayed alive long enough. As the first departing guest signals the break-up of a party, with Kar Sjontu's going they rose from the table. Shishu-Sji finished his wine at a gulp.

'Now I must practise my arts. I must seek to fathom this Zirmazd the Wily. You will be cared for. Kar Sjontu has given the necessary orders.'

'And Tara?'

'Your sister will stay here, under my protection. I guarantee you her safety, Torr Vorkun.'

'I accept,' said Torr, gravely, tall and commanding in the tent, yet feeling very alone among the Hosts of Sjombalku.

He slept that night in a small tent close by the wizard's. He kept Lycheaper naked by his side. Murgur's axe stood by the tent pole. The Sjombalkuans had brought his meagre belongings from the drynes, and the great horn bow he strung with a practised jerk and laid to his hand with the quiver. He trusted

Shishu-Sji – he had to do that – but in all, this great host there must inevitably be others of different kidney.

That night they were not disturbed. In the morning a Dentro guard, twitching his whiskers, waited for them, his falchion sheathed, to bring them to Shishu-Sji for breakfast.

His first words at the start puzzled then amused Torr.

'So you have been knocking nobles about – young nobles, who chafe at taking orders from older knights and who seek always to show off their prowess. The young dandies, they are called.'

'How is my sister?'

'She sleeps still. I shall keep her asleep for two more days, at the least. Her body was cruelly tortured.'

'Quapartz – '

'Think more of Wolfsbane and his kin! They seek to do you harm!'

'So he's here, is he.'

'Yes. I shall inform the Lord of the Earth and Thunder that I have a certain task for you. That should hold, in purely temporal terms, the lust for revenge of that ninny Wolfsbane.'

Shishu-Sji looked as though he hadn't slept all night. He picked up a golden robe to slip about his scarlet gown and, with his flat cap jammed down on his white thatch, he went out, turning at the tent flap to say: 'Keep to my tent. And, as you value your immortal spirits, touch nothing!'

'I am not unfamiliar with a wizard's chamber,' said Torr, casually.

'Humph!' sniffed Shishu-Sji, pre-eminent thaumaturge of the Hosts of Sjombalku, and went out.

From the tent flap Torr and Frelgar gazed on the morning bustle.

Here everything went forward with a snap and a drive that heartened the fighting spirit in him. These people had a purpose in life, the desire to find a new home, and their faces reflected that determination. He could respond to that, could Torr Vorkun of Darkholm. He contrasted the busy scene with that lack-lustre apathy of the castle of Gamelon Town.

'I'd take no bets on the Prefect's chances,' he growled.

'It's wizardry that will settle the issue,' reminded Frelgar.

'And Shishu-Sji will settle the issue,' reminded Frelgar. 'And Shishu-Sji seems a worried man to me.'

'Sorcery, mayhap. Swords, yes!'

Strings of teryxes cut the morning air. They saw squads of armoured men moving out to drill and exercise with weapons. This camp, they judged, must be moved on the line of march about once a week. That way the Hosts could leapfrog one another and maintain a steady onward impetus across the great plains of Garthland.

Kar Sjontu with two other heavily-muscled and scarred knights marched up. They wore a different kit today, heavier metal, plated as to front and back, with pauldrons and greaves, and with three pages, young lively lads with merry faces, carrying vast pot helms with gay plumes. The faces of the knights brought a sudden chill to Torr Vorkun.

The bracing morning air, the bustle, the bright faces of the young pages, the fluttering flags and banners, all abruptly melted at Kar Sjontu spoke.

'It is Wolfbane,' he said, harshly. 'He is raging for revenge. He claims it was not a fair fight; that you grasped his sword arm. I and my good companions, Kar Sjastry and Kar Sjoylem have no love for the dandies, for the petty nobility that decry good fighting men for their lack of Balku blood.'

'Aye,' growled Kar Sjastry, hewn from the same block as the others. 'We of the Sjomban line need no upstart claims to nobility.'

'They must chafe at their own insecurity, then,' remarked Torr, not really caring. He fretted to be allowed to see Tara, and reminded himself that sleeping she mended best of all.

'Wolfsbane has sent a challenge. In honour it must be met. We three stand together for you – '

'Now that is handsome of you,' said Torr, jolted back to reality. 'I welcome you, all of you, as my seconds – '

'Seconds, nothing! rapped Kar Sjontu. 'Wolfsbane brings six of his knightly friends. We fight alongside you!'

Bewilderment briefly took Torr Vorkun.

'But this is not your fight. And does the Lord of the Earth and Thunder allow private jousts within his Hosts?'

'Oh, aye, he allows it. That way every man keeps his fighting edge honed. That is our code of chivalry – you fight for your honour, or you tend the dung-pits of the Hosts' sjeeds!'

A jerk of the thumb indicated the animals ridden by the armoured men. Not unlike the horses of Drugay in body outline and shape, they cantered along on eight legs, slender as to fetlock, chunky as to gaskin, bushy tails held erect and insolently waving. Their necks, horse-shaped, ended in wide, squat, gape-jawed mouths with slender ears sharp pricked. Their coats were of varying hues, from near-black to chestnut to bay to near-white. Their eyes, large, luminous, intelligent, showed their mettle. They stood taller by several hands than the largest horse; and they looked to Torr Vorkun, that rapacious rustler of horse-flesh, excellent mounts for the fray.

'I see,' he chaffed. 'A messy job, by their size.'

'He's a cool one,' quoth Kar Sjoylem. 'You spoke a true word there, Sjontu!'

'We use sjeeds much as you must use those ridiculous bird mounts you had,' said Sjontu. 'We do not joust on teryxes, for they are too scarce and valuable for such sport.'

'So people get hurt, then, in these mock combats?'

'Mock combat!' roared the three knights. 'By Stasjofree! We fight to the death!' rumbled Kar Sjontu.

'But this is not your fight – and the rules of your tournaments are unknown to me.' Torr thought of various things, and then, his eyes not meeting those of the three knights, he added, in little more than a mumble: 'Cannot you beg this off?'

After he had quietened them down and soothed their ruffled chivalric feathers, he tried to explain, could not, decided he had best forget his qualms and let his own instincts take over. He touched the silver-wire wound hilt of Lycheaper. 'I am ready. Lead on.'

Frelgar put a hand on his arm.

'Torr – Shishu-Sji warned us not to leave the tent.'

'I know. But what would you have me do?'

'Then I join you –'

'No, good Frelgar. Do you stay here. Tara – the word from the chief of these people – remember, our lives hang by a brittle thread.'

He convinced Frelgar, who subsided, rumbling, and tramped off after the three knights and their pages. He felt, he had to confess, a trifle ridiculous; but he understood the demands of honour.

11

Sjeeds, Bronze and Naked Steel

'My honour is as impugned as your own,' growled Sjontu, 'in that I judged it a fair fight and the nobles of Balku challenge that. One day, when we have won our new home, there will be a reckoning among the hosts – '

'And I look on that day with sorrow,' grumbled Sjoylem.

In the sweaty dusty clangour of the arming booth Torr looked about on the armour provided him. Bronze breast and back, bronze cincture. Steel shoulder straps. Bronze mail here and there, bronze mail coif and bronze pot helm. He twitched the brave scarlet feather out irritably.

'Do you couch a lance and charge?'

'Aye. You have jousted before?'

'Seldom for fun.'

'In the mêlée after the first onset the fun dribbles away.'

'It is to the death, you said?'

'Aye.'

'So be it. Wolfsbane will find we have sharper teeth than any wolf he ever slew.'

'Bravely spoken, lad!'

Torr did not much like this armour-plating of himself for fighting, as though he were one of those clumsy turtles of the muddy islets in the Singing River. He preferred to feel free to wield the weapon to hand; but he saw the wisdom of armour to his back. This was civilised fighting; where rules had to be observed. But for his preoccupation with Tara's recovery, and his moody doubts over getting away from the Hosts of Sjom-balku at all, he might have joyed in the coming combat. As it was he just wanted it over – fast.

They mounted up. Like the borrowed armour, the borrowed

sjeed was of high quality. All a glowing chestnut, he stood, snorting softly, waiting to do his part of the coming duty to Valkur, God of War. They trotted gently out to the field, jingling as they went.

Torr sat the saddle lithely, holding the massive lance in couch, feeling the way the tip tended to weave tight spirals, knowing that the see-saw effect of a four-legged horse would be dampened out by the sjeed's eight legs.. He could attain a higher degree of accuracy in the charge, then. A marshal in brilliant colours over armour waved an arm, trumpets blew, people — many women and children — crowded to the wooden stockades thrown up around this place. The ground had been trampled by sjeed hoves before. The place smoked with a familiar smell. Lithely Torr sat, determined not to let the armour slow him down, drag on his sword arm.

From his saddle Murgur's axe swung. At his side scabbarded still in the old dragobrane leather. Lycheaper hung, as ever ready to flame into action. He'd smash the lance up and then get to close quarters. So he reasoned, beginning to drop back into his familiar habits of war.

Four knights similarly accoutred trotted into view at the far end of the field. They looked hard and dark and menacing.

Maidens dressed in parti-coloured dresses of blue and cerise danced out to them, bearing similarly-coloured favours and posies, ribbons which they garlanded the helmets of the four knights of Wolfsbane. So chivalry demanded equality in the shock on onset. Now other maidens, dressed in robes of orange and white, garlanded Sontu and Sjastry and Sjoylem. None of them offered to garland him, and for that he was savagely thankful.

The eight riders converged in the centre of the field and then, at a word from the marshal, turned to look up at the box overseeing the central expanse. On rugs and furs within the awninged box sat men, older men smiling to see youngsters at swordplay, women of high rank who smiled sickly-sweet on the knights below, youths and girls in bright gay clothes who smiled — with, was that soft sadness? Torr had no time to admire the inner politics of the Hosts now. At the side of a tough, grizzly man with a golden chain about his breast, sat a girl who suddenly, clearly, shockingly, jumped into focus for Torr Vorkun.

Seeing was not easy through the slitted visor of the pot helm; but Torr Vorkun could see this girl. He stared up hotly. All in white, she sat there, smiling, her small proud head held regally, the long dark hair flowing down, a posy of orange and white flowers in her hair. How to describe her in the wonder of that moment? Torr looked again, forgetting the fray to come, forgetting the sweating bronze tang of his helmet, the chafe of bronze mail, the noise and hubbub of the lists. The girl inclined her head to him.

'And is no maiden to give this outlander knight a favour?'

Carefully, she reached up and took down the orange and white flowers from her hair, held them out with one slim white arm. Stupidly, Torr looked and looked.

'Lower your lance, lad!' rasped the gonging voice of Sjontu from his helm.

Obediently, Torr lowered his lance. The girl slipped the posy on to the shaft. It slid down, came to rest on the vamplate. He had to leave it there. The extra weight and strength of the left-side armour, behind his shield, consisting of a clumsy elbow-reinforce and a wrapper for his left shoulder above the pauldron, together with his grip on the round and badly-designed shield, all prevented any movement save that of holding his body against the shock of the impact of lance on shield. If he was unlucky the lance would strike his helm. Riding a sharp course as they were, he did not relish that.

The posy clung, a splash of brave orange and white.

'Say your thanks, dolt!' rasped Sjontu. 'That is the lady Meline of Sjomba!'

Obediently, as though by rote, he said: 'Torr Vorkun of Darkholm of Drugay thanks my lady Meline of Sjomba for her favour.'

She cocked her left eyebrow at him, her pert mouth pouting with inner laughter, her face a glory before his eyes. 'And is that all, kar knight?'

'Observe the fight, my lady.' With that, before the others and bringing forth a few outraged snorts from the new people's gentry, Torr Vorkun wheeled his sjeed and trotted back to the

95

Sjomban end of the lists.

He had not failed to notice the great double-handed sword hanging at Wolfbane's saddle. The man was accustomed to the use of that weapon from the back of a teryx. In the dust and clamour and the heat of his armour, Torr Vorkun began to work up again to the man he really was, the man who had disappeared from the moment the Black Bodice had begun to constrict about Tara's waist.

They would be running a sharp course. He doubted if they used the tilt here. In the mêlée the end would come only by death. The savage spurting desire for bloody action took up Toor Vorkun then, so that once again he became the man the barbarians with whom he had taken Darkholm called Torr the Slayer.

The sjeed between his knees quivered as he scented the coming battle. He snorted, and tossed his head, and settled.

Without further preliminaries, on the sharp stridency of the trumpets, they charged.

Torr held his lance low, finding, as he had anticipated, the manoeuvring of the steel-tipped wooden shaft easier on eight-legged sjeed than on a four-legged horse. The hooves blended in their staccato rhythm, blood-poundingly, dust-spurting and kicking clouds from the churned-up ground behind them. The kick of the saddle against his rump and the weight of the armour set his blood afire. Chance had brought Wolfsbane against Sjoylem. Against Torr rode an unknown knight, wearing the blue and cerise, seeking to kill him.

The eight sjeeds coursed together like colliding seas within a rock-bound bight. Smashing clangour of steel on bronze racketted skywards. A sjeed shrilled in piercing agony. In the last second before he smote his man Torr Vorkun, leaning forward with all his weight behind his lance, deflected that tip of steel from the opposing shield and with unerring accuracy directed into the pot helm of his antagonist.

Whether he had ripped the man's head from his shoulders or not, Torr didn't know. He felt the smashing jolt of lance on his shield, saw the lance splinter into fountaining shards, rode on to haul up his snorting sjeed and wheel around for the next time.

Kar Sjoylem lay sprawled from his sjeed, whether dear or unconscious Torr could not see. His own man was down, still, blood gushing from the breaths and sights of his helm. Sjastry rode a few paces like a drunken sailor trying to negotiate the gangplank on a pitch-dark night; then his sjeed collapsed beneath him. His, then, the beast who had screamed.

Furiously, urging his mount on, rising and dipping to its surging, Wolfsbane bore down like an avalanche of metal on Torr Vorkun.

A vicious snarl drawing back from his lips, Torr wheeled his mount to meet him. He kicked the spurs into his sjeed's flanks, worked up a little speed and – smash – they came together.

Wolfsbane aimed for the helm.

Inclining his head clumsily, Torr slid the lance, crashed his own point directly into the round shield of his opponent. Like the topmast of a grounding galleon, the lance fractured and burst. Wolfsbane reeled back in his saddle, reeling, then lurching forward uncontrollably, skidded off his saddle and tumbled aheap on tó the muddy ground. A distant surf-roar from the stockade signalled a palpable smiting.

With a single comprehensive glance around the field Torr saw that he alone remained mounted. The other two of Wolfsbane's knights were down, one obviously dead – messily so – the other staring up at Sjontu's drawn sword hanging over his unhelmed head.

Deliberately, Torr dismounted.

He gripped black-thonged axe and walked, throwing down his shield, across to Wolfsbane. The Balku noble staggered up. Then, surprising Torr, he unbuckled the reinforces to his left elbow and shoulder, throwing them down with his abandoned shield. Seizing his long two-handed sword he sprang to meet Torr Vorkun.

At once Torr engaged. At a critical disadvantage with the bulky and movement-constricting reinforces of his left side he could not move as swiftly as Wolfsbane nor could he swing his left arm with freedom enough for what Murgur's axe required. Cursing his lack of knowledge of these people's customs of joust, he surged in, hacking and hewing.

The long double-handed blade flickered about him, donged against his pot helm. His head rang. How to contrive a defence with an axe? He sprang still closer in, and Wolfsbane, sensing victory, retreated, keeping that long sword circling. Twice Torr nearly had him, with blows that would have sheared of his head or shoulders, and twice Wolfsbane nearly thrust home in return.

The laws of chivalry of Vorkandalung – that far-off land of the gruesome serpent punishment pits – where Torr had first encountered the novel idea of rules of conduct governing fighting, dictated that a combatant might not resort to his next weapon until the one he was using was smashed. Did that apply here? Mockingly, Lycheaper swung against Torr's bronze-clad thigh.

Fighting instinct from his barbarian past proved the stronger in this moment of peril as the double-hander whistled down past his left shoulder. With a furious snarl Torr hurled the axe of Murgur straight at Wolfsbane. As the Balku noble ducked and dodged aside, Torr ripped at the latches of his reinforces. The metal plate dropped away. Then – then, to the accompaniment of a whoosed sigh of shivering excitement and vicarious horror from the spectators, Torr Vorkun reached up and drew off that ungainly pot-helm. That, too, he threw at Wolfsbane. The bronze flashed in the sun.

Wolfsbane let out a high yelping cry of pure triumph.

He rushed violently on Torr, the double-handed sword held high.

Lycheaper flamed.

The sweeping length of the two-handed sword whistled horizontally through the air in a blow aimed at making Torr's unarmoured head leap into the air. He evaded the blow with muscles trained in beast-fighting, snaked his own brand in. He struck at the base of the pot-helm. where it rested on the bronze breast. Wolfsbane's high yell of victory changed to a shrill yelp of pain as the helm clanged dizzyingly against his head. Again Torr smote him. And again. Now Wolfsbane staggered back, his left arm broken, his sword draggling. He tried to run and Lycheaper stroked all down his back so that he tumbled in a heap into the muddy earth.

Standing over him Torr wrenched off the pot-helm.

A vast soughing sigh broke from the watchers. A woman screamed. Men roared obscene jests and advice. Torr lifted his sword, not recking the cost now, thinking – aye, thinking in that moment of how his sister Tara, in mortal pain, had crawled to this man and salved and healed his wounds with her precious magic balm. He raised the sword. All his savage instincts impelled him to slice off the man's head without remorse.

With Lycheaper upraised, the din of the throng in his ears, he halted.

Above his head a small brown cloud grew into being.

The cloud broadened and now sparks shot through it, a ruddy glow spread, the scent of strange incense wafted down.

The crowd's noise diminished, dropped away into silence.

Through the sweat and dust and stink, gripping Lycheaper, Torr Vorkun stared up. The cloud blossomed into the awesome form of a man, a man of armour and of might, floating insubstantial there in mid-air. A massive voice blasted down.

'Stay your hand, Torr Vorkun! There is no need, now, for the final act of vengeance. Your honour is above reproach.'

That voice – surely, that was the voice of Shishu-Sji, magnified, strengthened, bellowing by magical arts into a godlike torrent of sound?

Slowly, Vorkun lowered his blade.

The sorcerer's voice lowered, whispered cuttingly.

'Did I not warn you stay within my tent?'

'There was knightly business afoot,' said Torr Vorkun.

'Maybe, maybe. But you have been sucked into the malignant squabbles between the Sjombans and the Balku. Go to my tent, at once, and stay there, as you value your life!'

Nursing his shattered arm, Wolfsbane glared up with a face that had taken on a macabre resemblance to a Dentro's.

'Your life is worth nothing to anyone any more, outlander!' The pain made him bite into his lip. When he could speak again, he whispered: 'I shall have you taken, never fear, to kill at my leisure!'

'As for you, Znunderbug-offal,' said Torr Vorkun lightly. 'If you pay other killers to kill as well as you, then I have nothing to fear.'

Shishu-Sji's magnified voice roared out again.

'Wolfsbane! Petty noble! This outlander's life is answerable to you! You know of the judgement of the Lord of the Earth and of Thunder! Beware lest you become a blot and a stench in his esteem!'

Wolfsbane lowered his face. He did not reply.

Sturdily, then, Torr Vorkun trudged across the churned ground, retrieved Murgur's axe. He shouted a coarse compliment to Sjontu, and was relieved to find Sjoylem nursing nothing more serious than a bruise and a headache.

'My thanks, good friends. It was good sport whilst it lasted.'

'Go now, Torr Vorkun,' commanded Sjontu. 'I will see to the armour and the sjeeds, all that is necessary to be done.'

'May Amadis be with you, Kar Sjontu.'

Then, very carefully, Torr went across to the shattered lance he had borne into the lists. He bent, picked out the small posy of orange and white. He felt its coolness. He tucked it into his old dragobrane leather belt.

He walked with his head high and and proud, his face hard, out from the place of jousting, through the crowd who murmured and stood aside from him, straight to Shishu-Sji's black tent of wizardry.

He did not rush that contemptuous passage – but neither did he loiter on the way.

His right hand hovered not very far from Lycheaper's silver-wire wound hilt.

12

My Lady Melina of Sjomba

Frelgar greeted him as though he had returned from the bowels of Sintian, or from the ice caverns of Black Nargoth himself.

'In Valkur's name!' growled Torr, shrugging off the Pragmatist's fear. 'Did you think a puppy like that could sink his puny teeth into this hriguara-proof hide?'

'Shishu-Sji was displeased, Torr – '

'As soon as Tara is recovered we leave here. I have business with Jaran the All-seeing.'

'As to that, Torr, talk with the wizard.'

'Oh?'

Frelgar would say no more. For the rest of that day they remained close in the black tent, served by the gossamer-clad maidens, replete with food and drink, yet with the itch to begone strong on them. Shishu-Sji did not put in an appearance. When the sun sank Dentro guards showed them to their own small tent which had been re-pitched beneath an extended black flap of the larger structure. On the ridge-pole a single crimson lamp burned, casting a glow that breathed menace down over the strained canvas.

'The Eye of Ehrenhale,' commented Frelgar, 'or whatever name the Sjombalkuans call it. Within that crimson glow we are safe.'

'More sorcery,' said the Drugayan, sourly.

'It can be used for good ends, as well as evil.' Frelgar sighed. 'Although I fear the latter predominate.'

About to retire they saw the tent flap lift and two tall grey-clad forms enter. Torr tensed – then relaxed as hoods were thrown back to reveal the laughing bright-eyed faces of young girls. Their long black tresses flew free as the hoods dropped.

Their cheeks shone. They twinkled with a conspiracy of merriment.

The younger held out a silver chalice in which warm ruby wine sent forth a spine-tickling aroma.

'Our mistress, the fair Lady Meline of Sjomba sends this as a good night drink, kar knights.'

She spoke more softly, then, conspiratorially. 'You are to take my sister's cloak, Kar Torr. You are to come with me. No one will know.'

A light like a bolt from Valkur's bow crashed into Torr's brain. He chuckled. He felt ripe for this adventure, by Amadis, the Goddess of Love herself!

Quickly, he donned the cloak, drew up the hood. The Pragmatist protested, jumping up, agitated.

'Nay, Torr! You know your dangers here – Shishu-Sji warned us – it is plain madness to venture into the camp at night – think, man, think! The Balku nobles –'

'I am thinking, good friend. I am thinking of white arms and white breasts, of red lips and dark eyes – she is a goddess herself!'

The two sisters giggled.

Ignoring Frelgar's further protests, Torr led out. As the girl turned to go, she said, saucily: 'My sister, Bettice, is to keep you company, Kar Frelgar. May you joy as Kar Torr will joy this night!'

'Go on, Patsy, you baggage!' scolded her sister, blushing.

The girl's height could be simulated by bending and in the grey close-drawn hood Torr passed by the Dentro guards and followed Patsy between the sleeping tents of the host until they reached a silver-cloth pavilion where shaded lights burned. He entered, his heart thumping, guided to a small rug-closseted space of rich furs and brocades, of golden vessels and sweet-smelling flowers, of a wide, low divan massed with golden-tasselled cushions. Reclining on the divan the lady Meline awaited him. Her face glowed with pleasure as he threw back the hood.

'Kar Torr! How – how I joy to see you!'

'My lady,' he said, bowing formally.

Patsy giggled and was imperiously dismissed.

Meline half-rose. She wore a transparent gown of silver cloth that revealed a form that dizzied Torr. She patted the place at her side and as he sat reached him a golden cup of warmed wine. The spicy odour enriched the savour of the moment. Her black hair lay about her shoulders, sprinkled with silver dust.

'You have brought your weapon, Torr . . .

He patted Lycheaper at his side. 'I count it a true blade, Meline . . . Today – I could not believe one so fair could exist . . . Your favour brought the victory – '

'And your manly strength – Torr – oh, Torr – I have waited long and lone for a true knight . . .'

He kissed her, the wine still wet on his lips, kissed her as a man in the desert after days of crazed wandering kisses the fountains from which flow life.

Gently he undid the silver thong bonding her robe, gently put it aside. She took him to her, pressing his head against her breasts, his hands guided to the firm roundness of her thighs, all the fire and blood in him blazing and scorching past reason.

When Patsy returned, giggling still, and guided him back to the tent within the protection of the Eye of Ehrenhale, he felt like a man drunk on the ambrosia that flows for the gods alone. By Amadis! What a girl!

Frelgar lay fast asleep, and Pettice was anxious to be gone. Drunk on his own thoughts, Torr lay long before he slept, not caring for Frelgar's conjectural exploits.

In the morning, when they had washed and breakfasted, Shishu-Sji summoned them.

'I will be brief,' he began without preamble. 'Your sister Tara has internal injuries that cannot be mended by touch, as I believe you know she can heal herself; and she will need a week at least. We move camp by then. Now – '

'She will recover?'

'Of a surety. My arts are not so fragile as to allow so wonderful a girl to perish – '

'I thank you, Shishu-Sji – '

The wizard waved that aside. 'Before I tell you what must be done, do you tell me – how is it that your sister can work small miracles of healing and yet for the deeper arts must strip? For the Black Bodice is known for its confining power on witches, great and small.'

Torr chuckled, relieved at the news. 'When we were small, scampering half-naked and like savages about the cave of our dear foster-father, Vorkun the Wise, he taught Tara the secret arts of healing and medicament. But of the blacker arts he would tell her nothing. Her small powers come from her illicit reading in his great tomes of thaumaturgical lore, quick glimpses when he was away. She practised on the tiny animals of the jungles below us, to the southwards. Soon she had amassed a stack of lore without dear Vorkun's knowledge; but his writ ran strong. She discovered that, like most witches, she had to be naked to enforce the witchery. We thought it was because she had read in the books as a naked wild little child.'

Shishu-Sji wheezed a chuckling laugh.

'It is a story the Lord of the Earth and Thunder will relish. But, now, for you, there is a task –'

Firmly, Torr Vorkun said : 'We must seek out Jaran the All-seeing –'

Shishu-Sji half-started back.

'Jaran! The mightiest wizard this world knows! Why?'

'You know of him! Zirmazd said he was dead; but that I will not believe. We travel westwards –'

'He is not dead. Tell me why you seek him –'

Excitement blazed up in Torr. 'Vorkun the Wise in his youth was famulus to Jaran the All-seeing. From him he learned his arts.'

'So!' breathed Shishu-Sji. 'Your foster-father was perhaps a greater man – a greater sorcerer – than perhaps you guess!'

'He was the greatest and the kindest and best man this world has ever seen!'

'Go on.'

'When we took Darkholm Vorkun needed its dry warmth and comfort, for his old cave in the Cargraiolf Mountains was damp and draughty and he had an illness on him nothing we could do would cure. At the end – at the end Vorkun wore an enchantment that slumbered him in a deep sleep. There he lies now, in ensorcelled sleep, awaiting the touch of Jaran the All-seeing to bring him back to young life again, vibrant and strong as we love him!'

'I see. But Jaran must see all this, he must know!'

'You mention the cause of my deepest fears. But Vorkun told us that Jaran intended to travel to the west. Tired of all his great powers, he vowed to find the place where the sun, the chariot of Father Uran the All-mighty, sank to rest. He vowed he would continue on to the west until he came to the place where the chariot of the sun is stabled. We follow him.'

'Gods!' sniffed Frelgar. 'The only god, is man.'

They ignored the Pragmatist.

Shishu-Sji wiped his dry lips and stared thoughtfully at Torr Vorkun.

'I will help you in your search, outlander. 'But — '

'I thank you, Shishu-Sji — I cannot hope to repay you for — '

'But,' went on the wizard, his voice deepening and taking on something of those sonorous tones his phantomed armoured image had projected on the field of joust. But you must aid me, of your goodness.'

'What?'

Torr Vorkun of Darkholm spoke stonily.

'I will tell you what is necessary tomorrow. I am in deep conclave with my familiar, Sjik. He is advising me how best to move against Gamelon. Sjorange, my old faithful familiar of many years, resents the intruder; but I have access to Gamelon!'

'Sjorange? Then you favour the Sjombans against the Balkus?'

Angrily, the wizard shook his head. 'I favour neither side in this malignant internecine strife! I am the wizard to the Lord of the Earth and of Thunder. Him I serve. He needs ghostly aid in this search for a new home for our people. For you must know that our own homeland was blackened and burned and destroyed for us by the baleful hosts of the winged yellow races, the Chans and the Tsings and the monstrous lizard-like Ngalugas!'

He quivered as he spoke, his old eyes spiteful and yet holding a strange and unsettling fear.

'They and their gods are accursed before the sight of men!'

As though the memory of horror overcame him, shuddering with remembered terrors, the wizard bade them begone and retired to the inner rug-enclose sections of his black tent.

That night once more Torr lay in the eager white arms of the lady Meline, joying alike in her passionate avowals and demands and the limber renewed strength of his own barbarian-thewed body. They made love as the first flames of the pyre leapt up, bright and clean and joyful, lusting after all sensation and all paradise.

Frelgar, muttering dire warnings, Torr disregarded. He could think only of the strong youthful pulse of blood within him, and of the white purity of Meline. How her red parted lips could drive him to a frenzy!

On the sixth day of this secret intrigue and of nightly passion, Shishu-Sji summoned them again.

Going into the black tent, Frelgar said forebodingly: 'Torr! This cannot go on! Your sister Tara is well again. You seek Jaran the All-seeing. Life is slipping you by and nothing is accomplished –'

'You are bored, Frelgar, that I know. Does not Pettice please you?'

'Aye. But there are other things in life besides white arms and breasts and the rest –'

'True. Meline is cloying, if lovable. But Shishu-Sji awaits word from Sjik his familiar –'

That word had come.

Shishu-Sji greeted them with a strange eagerness.

Kar Sjontu stood with him in the tent, scarred and grim; but lighting up with quick greeting at sight of Torr.

'I will not weary you with a recital of our internal politics, friend Torr.' Sjontu looked pleased. 'But the lady Meline's father is high in the favour of the Lord of the Earth and of Thunder. It may be, at last, as we prepare to assault Gamelon Town and then press on to reap a rich harvest in all the Land of Gamelon itself, that he will favour the Sjomban cause. The nobles of Balku howl like carrion-eating dogs! Hai – I spit in their faces.'

'The lady Meline,' said Torr, polite and cautious. 'I would convey my thanks and regard to her. As for the Lord of the Earth and of Thunder –'

Sjontu shook his head. 'He is a man overweighed with problems at this moment, Torr. As easily see him as see the ladies of his court in their baths!'

Torr laughed.

The silver double-bath of Meline had been sensuous last night with its fragrant warmed water – and yet, and yet . . .

'Tara?' he asked Shishu-Sji. 'How is my sister this morning?'

For answer a quick light silvery tinkle sounded beyong a hanging rug. The rug swept away and –

And Tara Vorkun of Darkholm stepped lithely into the sunshine, her face thrown back, laughing, her eyes bright. With a glad shout Torr swept her up into his arms, feeling her firm tawny strength against his, her dear arms about him, her cheek pressed against his. He put her off from him and looked at her.

'You are pale!' he said, accusingly.

She nodded, laughing still. 'But I am well, Torr, well again!'

She whirled a few light dancing steps, swirling the white gown with its orange embroideries about her lithe long legs. A light clicked on for Torr Vorkun, then, a resplendent brilliance of love.

He grabbed her again and kissed her, a brotherly kiss of affection and mutual joy. She felt good, did Tara Vorkun, firm and young and full-breasted, her long thighs and supply body bringing her brown hair level with his own.

'Well now!' chaffed Frelgar, pleased.

After the greetings, Shishu-Sji spoke of his familiar, simply, without any necromantic trappings.

'Sjik informs me through his nightmare world of the pits that if we can introduce a certain – a certain something – into Gamelon Town, I can use it to focus all my powers therein.'

Frelgar huffed, and stood looking at Tara. She continued to hang on Torr's left arm.

'Your word on Zirmazd was a good word. Sjik has infiltrated that doddering sorcerer's chamber, bypassing my efforts against the Quapartz the Bloody-handed.'

'I have not forgotten him!' quoth Torr Vorkun grimly.

'All that now remains to be done, as the Hosts of Sjombalku march against the evil of Gamelon, is for you, Torr Vorkun, to take that certain something into Zirmazd the Wily's chamber!'

So this was the payment, then.

Vorkun of Darkholm nodded.

'I have a certain power with Zirmazd, a power gained by the point of my true blade Lycheaper. By Valkur! I will do it, and in the doing cleanse my spirit of the affront so callously afforded us in the pits of Gamelon Town!'

With a true barbarian's contempt for the right and wrongs of a case, he dismissed the chicken. He would have bartered, by the world-spinning guts of Obese Rumphaldi Himself! He would have bartered fairly.

'So be it, then. Our arts of disguise can easily turn your brown hair red, where our own young men's black hair flows long and betrayingly.' The wizard sighed. 'They risk mutilation and death rather than cut their hair, the badge of their prowess!'

'And brown hair streaked with grey?' asked Frelgar.

Tartly, Torr snapped: 'You mean grey hair streaked with brown, you vain Pragmatist you!'

'Were I not foresworn to my vows – were I still Frelgar the – by the mercy of man to man, young Torr Vorkun, I'd spell you into a mealy-bug this instant!'

They all laughed.

Yes, they all laughed, and yet, Torr Vorkun knew, the task ahead of them was no light one, easily performed, like slipping into a lady's tent o' nights.

That night he sipped passionately of the lady Meline's charms. He overwhelmed her with his demands. And yet, as he returned to the tent with Patsy, he shuddered and wondered at himself. So cool, she had seemed, and so fiery with passion – and yet, and yet . . .

How he looked forward, by the sweet breath of fair Amadis the Goddess of Love herself, to riding out in the morning with his sister, Tara of Vorkun of Darkholm, laughing at his side!

13

The Mirth of Quarpatz the Bloody-Handed

'May the gods of Sjombalku fly with you!' intoned Shishu-Sji the wizard. 'May Tzorisj and Stasjofree and Dalku-Darm extend their winged comfort and sustenance to you in this your endeavour.'

The teryxes took off in a battering of wings, fluttering dust beneath the morning sunshine. All about the Hosts of Sjombalku folded their tents and set about the last and triumphant march upon the land of Gamelon. High into the bright keen air the teryxes winged, strong pinions carrying their riders buffetting against the wind, their scarlet-clawed feet clamped beneath their bodies, joying in their high freedom from the muddied earth beneath.

Far to the north they winged, across the wide-flung plains, leaving the long wending lines of the host to sink below the horizon in their eastward march, until they came to the rim of the Opal Sea, where white waves flung themselves on a golden shore and small bushes blew in the sea breezes and the sun sparked flashes of fire from the tumbling waters.

Turning eastwards they flew untiringly through the still noon-day heat, refreshing themselves with water and biscuits on the wing. Towards evening Kar Sjontu in command of the escort which included faithful Sjastry and Sjoylem, and Sjiri and Sjallu, pointed down. Down there where the shadows of evening gathered about the estuary of the Singing River they saw the first flickering uncertain lights sparkling up from scattered hamlets and lonely crossroad inns. Some shipping on the river pulled in for the night, to resume the short journey to Gamelon Town on the morrow. Torr could sense an unease about the night, a feeling that great unseen forces were moving against the March of Gamelon that buffered all the Lands of Gamelon beyond. Truly, out of Garthland had come a host of vengeance.

They leaguered that night among the reeds and mud of the estuary where night birds called and the click and scurry of nocturnal life rustled through the narrow water channels. The moon rose and cast many fragmented runnels of silver across the waters. They lit no fire, ate cold victuals, and wrapped themselves in furs and rugs.

Strangely enough, the most trouble came from the three drynes, the same beasts they had ridden from Gamelon Town and which had been brought into the Hosts' camp by Sjiri and Sjallu with the venom-inflamed Wolfsbane. The drynes' bronze-studded red-velvet trappings over their cruel beaks had to be tight drawn. Clearly, the land-bound birds disliked flying. The teryxes ruffled their feathers and brought out a weird animosity from bird to flying beast.

After a short rest and long before betraying morning broke Kar Sjontu and his comrades said their goodbyes. Their teryxes took off in muted wing-thunder, and the three left below waved until the shadows engulfed them.

With the light they mounted the drynes and set off through muddy tracks and near-swamped pathways towards the high stone road flanking the river and – Gamelon Town.

'May the Mace of Moray strike the place to rubble!' said Torr Vorkun as they saw the long grey battlemented walls come into view, with the forbidding castle towering above, its many flags and guidons flying in the morning breeze.

'They have been reinforced since we have been away,' observed Frelgar. He looked ten years younger with his hair dyed a Gamelon red.

'Aye. Cavalry, by the look of yonder guidons. No matter. Sjombalku will crush them!'

'But only if we can put that casket thing into Zirmazd's chamber,' warned Tara.

Torr touched the bulge beneath his fawn tunic. Like them all, he had been outfitted in what seemed suitable for a simple country gentleman of the Lands of Gamelon. He kept his old dragobine belt and scabbard and his boots. Tara, accepting the corlish leather tunic, well tailored to cover her bound breasts into manlike shape, had wanted nothing of her old boots, despite that they had been cobbled from the same hide as Torr's, the famous dragobrane celebrated in Grendan's song, the Lord High King's harper of golden melody. She remembered too well the indignity they had caused her.

'Only the buckles, dear Tara. The buckles only!'

But she had been adamant and now rode with a pair of low-cut soft-leather boots in Sjilkish hide, and swore they were becoming enough for the gallant blade she aped. Frelgar kept his own counsel.

Torr thought of that last night with Meline, of her tears and supplications, and of his own embarrassment and feelings of disgust. She had wanted him so badly. He glanced across at Tara. A she-witch, a girl with a mind of her own, that would tell her high-and-mighty brother what to do and how to do it to the best self-mocking affect she might be; but she was Tara. Tara! He would not give a week's dalliance with all the Meline's in the world for one fond glance from Tara's eyes.

Later on, as they swung rhythmically along on their drynes on the stone high road, they began arguing about their chances of escaping detection. Frelgar harrumphed with despairing humour. Finally, when they were glaring at each other, their heads high, their proud Vorkun noses in the air, their cheeks hot, he tried to interrupt.

' . . . you will not!' Torr was shouting.

'And so I will, you great big puffed-up heap of impudence!'

'I go alone into Zirmaxd's chamber, witch!'

'Little brother — I am sworn to care for you — I, too, go into the wizard's lair; if you insist on accompanying me, so be it.'

'Little brother!' Torr gobbled his outrage. 'I am older than you! Obviously so —'

'Obviously I am the elder! My common sense makes that inevitable!'

'You're not! I am!'

'I am!'

'I'll — I'll take your pants down and tan your backside red!'

'Oh, the gallant knight! And what happened the last time you tried that?'

111

Torr hiccoughed, raging. 'That wasn't fair! You – '

Tara tinkled her mocking laugh. 'No! And I'll do it again if you dare!'

'Witch!'

'Brainless barbarian sworder!'

Frelgar shouldered his dryne between them, wondering if they'd notice him, wincing from their heat.

'I suppose you've argued thus a hundred times,' he said. 'But if you were abandoned as you say, why, then you cannot know who was the first born, can you?'

Torr and Tara glanced at him, befuddled by the temper of them that had flashed like summer lightning.

'So!' the Pragmatist finished for them. 'It makes no difference, does it?'

'Maybe not. But Tara knows when I mean what I say!'

'And Torr had better know I mean to go into Zirmazd's skull chamber with him!'

'As for that,' Frelgar said grimly. 'We have a few days to establish ourselves in the town. We had best see to our plans without arguing about the first born of a pair of hot-tempered, intemperate, loud-opionated and stupid god-believing twins as I've ever come across in a long and evil life!'

The Vorkuns glared at the Pragmatist, who returned their simmering gaze with a calm and lofty indifference that maddened them all the more. By the time they reached the gateway to Gamelon Town, from which they had last ridden past an ensorcelled sentry sleeping over his halberd, they had only partially resumed their normal converse. Truly, chuckled Frelgar to himself, they were a right pair of – of – And then his Pragmatist's mind quickened to the gush of pure joy he relished in his discovery of these twins. They had brought a savour to life he had long thought vanished for ever.

The wizard of the Sjombalku host had made sure the bags of gold they had filched in payment from the Prefect's chamber had been placed on their mounts, so now they could pay for decent lodgings. From motives of concealment they lodged separately, Frelgar and Tara posing as father and son, and Torr as a country gentleman up to see the coming fight and take part against the invasion from Garthland. There were many such in the town, swaggering about swinging their swords and boasting, wearing gorgeous ludicrous uniforms. There were also many more soldiers, of various regiments and with a strong cavalry arm.

From all the provinces and petty dukedoms away up to the north along the eastern border of the Opal Sea men and weapons flowed in to the March of Gamelon. From the eastward and all the dependent kingdoms to the north of the Singing River as it flowed on its meandering north-westerly course to the wedge-shaped intrusion of the Opal Sea at its estuary rode men hungering for the chance of meeting these new black-haired people out of Garthland.

Many and many a time Torr heard the name of Black Nargoth invoked. He heard the blasphemous name of Quapartz the Bloody-handed banded about with obscene jests as to the fate of captured maidens. He saw, with a pang, the bodies of youths hanging with mutiliated and ruptured forms at the corners of streets. Their black long hair flowing down their tortured bodies bore traces still of that red dye so useless to them.

Everywhere there was bustle and movement, the rapid passage of dryne patrols, the rumbling rolling of cart after cart loaded with the provisions of war, the drilling and marching of the men in puce and bronze, their white cloaks flaring. And, too, there were other regiments, clad in bronze and blue, bronze and crimson, all with the proud white cloak of Gamelon billowing about them. A civilised, disciplined, orderly regime, that of Gamelon, even if its civilisation brought a chill of revulsion to the savage heart of a barbarian from the wild broken lands of Drugay.

No Eye of Ehrenhale watched over him now.

Within the first two days the three companions established the routine of the castle and estimated they had sought out the best means of ingress that would give them at least the chance of a trained thief to reach the tower where Zirmazd's skull-shaped chamber awaited them.

Lohr Prendil, the prefect, led a regiment past their lodgings on the third day and the people roared their approval from the mud-splashed boards. Bravely the drynes paced, their riders in their puce and bronze erect and grim-faced, their lances all aslant in the sun.

Vorkun studied the face of Prendil, and smiled a vicious smile. For the Prefect's face bore still the swollen traces of his incarceration in the iron body-formed cage and the iron-gag thrust so violently into his mouth. He spoke graciously to his people; but his was a gap-toothed smile.

When they had been in the town a week and had agreed on their plans — with a plentitude of further acrimonious wrangling as to who was the first born of the Vorkun twins — a flame of rumour ran through the narrow streets. Then the facts were confirmed. The new people out of Garthland had been seen, riding like a black cloud across the land!

The long-awaited invasion was at hand.

With martial pomp and jingle and clatter of bronze and steel the many-coloured regiments marched out. Rank after rank of them swung through the west gate, proudly stepping out to challenge the black-haired might. Their whole bearing and demeanour had been worrying Torr. He stood to watch them go, knowing he must act now, and yet, and yet —

'They have their fighting spirit back,' he said uneasily to Frelgar, who held one arm familiarly on Tara's shoulder. 'They were dismayingly unlike the cowed wretches we dealt with when we broke from the castle.'

'Aye,' said Frelgar shortly.

'Mayhap their sorcerers have put false heart into them,' suggested Tara. 'As, father mine, Shushi-Sju will have inspired the hearts of all Sjombalku.'

'It all depends on which side you look at it,' said Torr. 'But, of course, Frelgar our Pragmatist friend will have none of that.'

'If the sorcerers of either side lose their ghostly combat, then nothing of swords or steel will save their earthly followers.' Frelgar look his disgust at the conception. 'It is foolish; but it it true because men in their folly believe it to be true.'

'By Valkur! You deny what your eyes tell you is so!'

'My eyes may tell me what I see; but my mind tells me that I see what is not so — '

Tara broke the encroaching squabble.

'We had best go now. Once the battle is joined all our

114

efforts will be needed. Remember what Shishu-Sji said.'

Silently, they swung through the excited streets of Gamelon Town towards the castle and the chamber of Zirmazd the Wily. Now they faced the payment of their debts.

The idea had crossed Torr's mind that it would be wise for them to ride on, at first southerly and swinging around the Hosts of Sjombalku, until they could resume their westerly progress; but a greater wisdom told him that sure death, sure retribution, would follow that folly.

A debt to a wizard of however fair-minded a kind was a debt. And debts could be collected in blood.

Armed only with their swords and with main-gauche daggers of gilt-steel Zushite work, they marched boldly into the frowning entrance of the castle's main gate. The sentries on duty were mainly older men and raw recruits, those who could be spared with little loss from the battalion companies marching bravely out to battle. The air of tension everywhere sparked quick emotions, raw reactions.

'By Supernal Tremineds himself!' roared Torr Vorkun. 'Must I answer to a jackanapes schoolboy when I have pressing business within!'

The young sentry hesitated – and Torr pushed past with a menacing curse that drove the blood from the immature face. The halberd, seeming too unwieldy for those narrow shoulders, snapped back at attention. The three companions strode into the castle of Gamelon Town.

How they remembered this vile place!

Torr ran his keen glance raking along the ramparts. The tower of the Prefect, the tower within which lay Prando the Unsleeping's chamber, the tower of Zirmazd for which they aimed – oh, yes, he remembered!

Clanking their booted feet down arrogantly, they marched up the staircase, came out on to the battlemented ramparts. Everything went ahead smoothly. They neared that well-remembered door, through which they had gone but from which they had not emerged.

Torr fingered the jade casket ready to hand within his unlatched tunic. 'Guard that with your life!' Shishu-Sji had told them. 'For if it falls into the wrong hands – aiee! It is

115

my doom no less than that of Sjombalku!'

He wondered what could lie nestled within that casket of jade that meant so much, both to Gamelon as to Sjombalku. Sorcery, without doubt. His fingers slid away from the smooth jade, repelled by the thought. If Frelgar could read his mind now, how that old Pragmatist would mock . . .

Tara flung him a quick, bird-like glance of concern and reassurance, and at once he cursed himself, and took again the attributes of Torr the Slayer. They reached the door.

A black crow bird flapped rusty wings and flew croakingly with a harsh rasping screech from the battlements.

This time a guard had been posted at Zirmazd's door. A gruff-faced soldier wearing chequered puce and black tunic and bronze mail, he drew his scimitar menacingly, waving it at them. A thump of relief hit Torr Vorkun as he drew his sword and leaped in. He despatched the sentry without a pause, with barbarian-like suddenness, and eased open the door on to that skull-chamber of wizardry.

So silent had he been, so quick and pantherish, that he was into the chamber Zirmazd the Wily, entranced in his sorcerous magic, could comprehend. The guard, posted to detain and warn, had died too quickly.

The familiar charnel stench flowed from the scarlet and black pentacle. There crouched the revolting toad-thing from the pit, Lunga-Tuchulchya, smoke wreathing his hollow eye sockets, croaking wheezily at his master.

' . . . for all his arts he cannot approach you, honoured master, for black devilment and vile intrigue within the ghostly lands of the pit.'

Zirmazd the Wily, pushing back his toppling conical cap, chuckled like those fish-eating birds of the Nefrayle Lakes, when they screech down to pluck out the eyes of their victims.

'That is good, most good, Lunga-Tuchulchya. And soon they will be here. Calls you Sjik, does he! Oh, by the sport of Black Nargoth with the maidens of Primotur's harem! I like this well! It comforts my old bones now I have lost the golden egg – and that may not be altogether –'

The rambling, wheezing, chuckling voice died on a gurgle as Torr Vorkun smashed into the chamber.

116

Lunga-Tuchulchya screeched. 'This one knows I am also Sjik! He must be torn to pieces —'

But through the horror of the deadly revelation, a fresh horror hit Torr Vorkun. About to shout a venemous reminder to Zirmazd that his promise not to harm the Vorkuns still held, Torr froze.

From the shadows beyond the brazier a squat man with a red spade beard and eyes that reflected the blood-red light like coals from the furnaces of Sintian moved like a creeping terror from a nightmare.

'They have brought the casket from Shishu-Sji! Now we have the hair and skin and nail-parings of the chief sorcerer of the Sjombalku in our hands! Oh, Lunga-Tuchulchya, you have done well! Sjik has betrayed his new master most blasphemously well!' Quapartz the Bloody-handed guffawed his evil intent. 'Now are all the Hosts of Sjombalku betrayed into our hands! Now can we rend them utterly into pieces!' He nodded almost indifferently at the Vorkuns and Frelgar.

'As for these three — Black Nargoth may take them and do with them what deviltry he wills!'

14

Torr the Slayer

That evil skull-shaped chamber spun dizzyingly in Torr's sight. The alembics and the vials and jars gleaming with all the colours of hellfire with their thaumaturgical contents, the wired skeletons, the ponderous tomes of alchymical lore, the blasphemous root of the wombscrawn tree, the smoke and stench from the braziers, the sound of Zirmazd's eerie chuckle and the bellowing confident boom from Quapartz, all blended into a mind-paralysing poison.

Now all the gay hosts of Sjombalku were doomed! The armoured cavalry riding so bravely on their caparisoned sjeeds, the flying wedges of teryxes, the long lines of covered wagons and marching men and women, the plain-blackening herds of cattle, all, all would be engulfed by the puce and bronze of the Land of Gamelon!

Gruff gallant Kar Sjontu and his comrades, the Lord of the Earth and of Thunder, the lady Meline of Sjomba, all would descend to unknown suffering in the ice caverns of Black Nargoth. And Shishu-Sji – the chief wizard, he who had trusted the Vorkuns to be his agents – what of him? With the scraps of his hair and skin, the parings of his nails, that nestled within the jade casket he had hoped to bring triumph to the Hosts. Instead, they would bring his devilish enslavement and lingering death.

For less than a single heartbeat Torr Vorkun of Darkholm stood glaring on his fate.

He possessed the dazzling lethal speed of a barbarian, the stealthy killing swiftness of a jungle beast, and his mightily-thewed body had grown hard and enduring through hours of rock-climbing and in the shock of battle. His instincts were those of fierce and insensate hate, forcing him to act immediately and without recking the cost, making of him a savage and sudden instrument of destruction. But, over-riding all these attributes of barbarism he possessed the cool calculating mind of a civilised man, shrewd and judging, capable of flexibility and of knowing when to allow Vorkun of Darkholm to rule and when to allow Torr the Slayer to lash forth in unbridled fury.

Confronted thus with all the apparatus of the sorcerer's art, conscious of demonology and of the fate ordained for him, a simple barbarian would have remained rooted, unable to move, his mind a frozen terror-filled block. But Torr Vorkun was no longer a naïve barbarism confronted with the supernatural.

No, by Valkur! He was Torr Vorkun of Darkholm of Drugay!

And – he was also Torr the Slayer!

Less than a single heartbeat had passed.

Tricked and trapped by these wizards he might have been, gulled by the treachery of Lunga-Tuchulchya who had persuaded Shishu-Sii in the guise of Sjik to send a body-hostage of himself into the clawed hands of these sorcerers, awaiting a hurtling spell that would spin him and Tara and Freigar down into the ice caverns of Black Nargoth, all these things remained so. But, equally remaining so, wizards of high repute and thaumaturges of awesome power, Zirmazd the Wily and Quapartz the Bloody-handed yet remained men with old and sluggish reflexes and reactions. The gods might speak through them, and demons and devils; but they acted with ordinary human speed.

Wrapped up in the evil power of their coming victory and vaunting their own praises in the prideful words, taking diabolical pleasure from the stricken mortals who faced them, they moved their muscles with the slow painfulness of slothful living and city-bred reactions.

Torr the Slayer struck!

The hot savage rush of barbarian blood and the mind-numbing speed of his beast-like reactions nerved him now.

The gilt-steel Kushite main-gauche dagger flashed like a bolt from Szangkill the Archer across the chamber.

Chokingly, with his hand upraised to blast an enchantment, and with the gilt-steel hilt protruding from his throat, Quapartz the Bloody-handed tried to speak, tried to chant the spell that would blast these puny humans down into the ice caverns of Black Nargoth. But his vocal cords had been shattered. The black ichor poured foaming from his throat.

He reached up, clawing and grasping, choking and gurgling most terribly. But he did not fall.

'Stand back, Zirmazd!' rapped Torr. 'Remember your sworn oath! Break it at your peril, for I know you fear Primotur of the Lightnings!'

In a ghastly parody of death Quapartz struggled about the chamber, spreading a slime of black blood over everything near him.

'The victory was ours!' wailed Zirmazd. 'Now my Supernal Tremineds aid us now!'

The jade casket against Torr's breast warmed, heated, glowed. He could feel its pulse against his heart. He knew that Shishu-Sji was trying to break through the bonds of wizardry guarding this chamber. But still Quapartz struggled and lurched about gurgling a ghastly retching croaking. And now – and now!

And now things – blasphemous things, obscene things – grew from the flailing form of Quapartz. Snake-headed lions, and toad-headed serpents, writhed hissing from his form. Fanged mouths opened.

The confines of the chamber receded so that it seemed to Torr Vorkun that he trod the insubstantial mistiness of clouds sailing over the plains of Garthland. Even as he drew Lycheaper and struck viciously at the solid phantasms that sought to destroy him, he was aware of the hosts below.

The keen blade sliced through scaly flesh, severed frog heads and lion heads, cut and slashed. Yet more and still more obscene horrors flowed from the writhing form of the dying sorcerer.

'By Chomath the Defiled! Die, you cess-pit of evil!'

And now armoured men issued from the mangled form of Quapartz, misty with glints of bronze armour, solidifying, thickening into giants of war who threw themselves roaring on

120

to Lycheaper's blade. Desperately there he struggled, balanced insubstantially between earth and sky, his blade jolting to the all-too solid thunk of return blows.

Keening voices shrilled from the phantasms conjured by the necromancer in this final great trial.

'Supernal Tremineds! Black Nargoth!' The voices screamed like the whirlwind as it plucks houses into its whirling blackness and lies waste to the cities of the plain.

Then a new voice entered the uproar, a voice that Torr knew – the voice of Shishu-Sji, speaking to him by virtue of the body-hostage within the jade casket glowing against his breast!

'Stand fast, Torr Vorkun! For I cannot reach you now – the trickery has been blacker than the blade of Dalku-Darm!'

A bronze-clad giant smashed forward brandishing a huge axe like unto that axe taken from Murgur, brought the keen blades down in a mighty overhand sweep that would have cloven Torr in two. He skipped aside and Lycheaper flamed in and the giant reeled back with phantom blood pouring from the severed stump of his arm. The axe vanished. But more and more monsters poured screaming and shrilling across the insubstantial cloud platform, ravening to tear down the limber form of Torr Vorkun and his lethal blade.

'How much longer?' grunted Torr, hacking and thrusting.

'The strength of Gamelon is now pitted against the Host of Sjombalku! All across the plains armies clash in war!'

Fragments of that earth-bound battle reached Torr's sight as he battled supernatural forces in the upper air. Hordes of puce and bronze cavalry, their white cloaks flying, charged with serried ranks of Sjombalku. Roaring avalanches of sjeeds coursed smashingly into the Gamelon regiments. Steel and bronze winked and flamed, down there, on the plain of Garthland, where the fate of empire hung in the balance – No, by Vulkur! No – the fate of Gamelon and of Sjombalku was being decided here, here in this hazy mid-air realm of supernatural horror where Torr struggled against demon-created phantasms directed through the form of Quapartz the Bloody-handed!

For, Clearly, Torr saw that as he lopped a serpent head, as he thrust out the eyes of a fang-slavering monster, so the ranks of puce and bronze below were shattered and fell back, reeling.

And when a lion-bodied dragon-fanged monster nicked his arm to bring the bright blood oozing, below a charge of sjeed cavalry faltered and went down beneath the bows of Gamelon's archers!

As he prevailed, so did the men of Sjombalku; and when he faltered and fell back, so Gamelon surged forward, roaring the victory!

The gods of the nations fought together through the agency of Quapartz and his sorceries and of Torr and his sword.

Lycheaper flamed and flamed aagin. Yet unendingly the armoured giants and the monsters and the chimerae poured gibbering from Quapartz upon him. Unable to cast a spell the sorcerer could not hurl him into the demon pits; but he could still call on the help of his gods to battle the fighting barbarian on his own terms.

'I have called on help,' wheezed that ghostly whisper from Shishu-Sji in his mind. 'Tzorisji and Stasjofree sustain your arm, kar knight! But the battle is in your hands! Fight – fight. for more than our lives, for your life, the life of your sister and your friend – fight for your very spirit's sake!'

Desperately, feeling the fatigue dragging on him, the weakening lassitude, stealing over his muscles as his blood leached away, Torr Vorkun of Darkholm fought on.

Down below on the plain the armies of Gamelon and of Sjombalku clashed in earth-shaking battle. But all their valour and all their gallantry meant nothing beside the simple courage of the Drugayan battling within the misty confines of that supernatural ampitheatre of the sky.

Red blood and black ichor coated the footings, for all that they were the gossamer ledges of clouds floating in the air. Recklessly, Torr surged in, slicing and hewing; yet cautiously he placed his feet for each blow with the instinctive feeling for balance native to him.

Then he noticed a strange and weird thing, to him as wonderful as anything that had gone before.

For as he struck the bronze armour his good sword Lycheaper did not nick; the steel sliced the bronze without blunting. He had refused Kar Sjontu's offer and instead of letting the knight's armourers hammer out the dint in the blade of Lycheaper, caused when he had smashed the iron lock of that iron cage that – by Chomath the Defiled! – stood here in this very chamber where he knew by all of sanity he must battle, he had himself carefully tapped out the nick and sharpened up the edge, watchful of the temper.

Now he struck more shrewdly, aiming with a master-swordsman's care, severing serpent body and serpent head with single, economical blows. For all along his giant thews and corded muscles the deadly fatigue crept and cramped and sought to pluck his body down into the deathly sleep of complete oblivion. He fought the supernatural manifested in grotesque and hideous forms with all his powers of swordplay.

A taloned claw licked out to gash his calf. A downward, half-timed blow, severed the clawed horror. He danced back, then swered to avoid a double-handed sword's blow, sank Lycheaper into the bronze mail of the apparition, jerked it out. More writhing, tentacular, slimed horrors of nightmare groped towards him, hissing.

'How much longer, Shishu-Sji?'

'Until the end, Torr! Until the end!'

Another mailed giant wielding another simulacrum of Murgur's axe whirled towards Torr. Defiantly, he surged up to meet the rush. Built to be swung one handed by the giant, the axe, too short to be the parallel to the long two-handed danheim axe that could weave a circle of hissing death about its wielder, this axe nevertheless for a few moments held Torr off. Then he flung forward, slid beneath the double-bitted head, slashed Lycheaper in a diagonal blow that crushed shoulder-joltingly through the giant's neck. Bits of spinning bronze, blood and bone cascaded.

'Keep at them, Torr!' Shishu-Sji's wheezing voice echoed in Torr's skull. 'Quapartz cannot do more now than send these solid apparitions against you; he has lost his power to command the deeper sorcery. His blasphemous gods give him this power – but that is all! Fight, Kar Torr! Fight!'

'By Chomath the Defiled,' the words barely brushed Torr's bruised lips. 'What d'ye think I'm doing?'

On the dust-smoking plains below the long steady lines of Gamelon puce and bronze, and blue and bronze, and red and bronze with the white cloaks swirling advanced against the very

123

wagon trains of the Hosts of Sjombalku. Vainly squadrons and wedges of teryxes hurled down from the sky, javelins hurtling, arrows darting, vainly seeking to halt that disciplined onward stamp. Low over their sjeeds necks the knights of Sjombalku hurled themselves on those serried ranks. The air darkened with arrows. Men and animals roared their pain and anger. Defiantly, fighting fiercely and savagely, the warriors of Sjombalku were pressed back.

A ghastly wheezing bubbling laughter welled from shattered vocal cords around the gilt-steel hilt. The black ichor sprayed now slowly and yet more slowly from the bitter wound.

Sweat stung into Torr's eyes. His body glistened with drenched blood and ichor. His sword arm rose and fell with a waning vigour; yet he fought on, fought on it seemed for hour after hour as the battle swung to and fro beneath him.

After all this – he could not fail now!

'Die, you blasphemous carrion-thung!' he growled, the words chopping bloodily past bruised lips.

A whole uprearing monstrous head, as large as a house, with curved horns seeking his vitals, with slicing fangs seeking his throat, with a baleful green steam issuing from scarlet and black nostrils, bent over him, crushingly.

He flung up Lycheaper.

'What do I care for these pantheons of pagan gods!' he screeched at the shade of Shishu-Sji there in his skull. 'By Valkur and by Chomath the Defiled! There is only one god in all the world! And I call on him now – aid me, Father Uran the All-mighty! Aid me now!'

Lycheaper flamed into destructive violence, biting and biting with keen stained blade into that descending monstrous head. Horns flew, fangs clashed, a fuming ichor engulfed him so that his lungs scorched. Surrounded by the fire and smoke billowing from the monstrous infernal head, Torr of Vorkun battled on, struggling when it must seem all struggle futile, the battle lost.

He felt the fangs close on his left arm . . . A wicked horn transfixed his thigh . . . A clawed tentacle looped from the fiery smoke and gashed into his shoulder . . .

Below him, the sjeeds toppled back, their riders falling . . .

The teryxes dropped flapping from the air, their proud bodies transfixed by Gamelon shafts . . .

But still Torr struggled. Again and again he thrust Lycheaper at the multiple eyes knotted between bony brows. Disgusting fluids dropped like acid, searing his flesh. He struck again and again, the muscles coiling across his back and shoulders, ridging into gleaming and shadow-bordered cables along his arms, staining like the thews of Valkur himself up his legs and thighs.

The monstrous head drooped. The eyes darkened. A haze descended – and, through that haze, he saw the form of Quapartz the Bloody-handed, saw him all enveloped in quivering violet light. The pain crushing his body as though he lay pressed between the iron ribs of the iron maiden herself came near to paralysing him. He felt the leaden weights dragging at his feet, his legs, his knees . . .

He swung up Lycheaper and felt the blade scarce respond to the last quivering orders from his muscles –

A voice resounded brazenly in his mind.

'Remember, Torr Vorkun of Darkholm! Remember the Black Bodice!'

With a last desperate surge of will-power Torr threw all the strength he had left into one final feral spring, one last blow from Lycheaper.

Quapartz the Bloody-handed's head sprang from his shoulders, spouting black ichor, to bound and roll upon the stone floor of Zirmazd's skull-shaped chamber!

Torr lowered the point of his sword to the flags and leaned. Smothered with his own blood, he saw the black ichor fume and vanish, the reassemblance of the tower chamber about him. He leaned and sucked in great draughts of air with agonised labouring.

And – and on the plain the Hosts of Sjombalku raged forward, levelled lances smiting the regiments of Gamelon into the dust. Clouds of arrows darkened the sun, flung javelins pierced corselets and mail and leather. The battering onslaught of sjeeds trampled down the puce and bronze and the proud white cloaks lay mired in the ground of the plain of Garthland. Like the foaming sea as it dashes up a rocky beach and flings itself into the sheltered cove beyond the hordes of Sjombalku drove exultantly over their fallen foes.

'Now praise be to Tzorisj and to Stasjofree!' said the voice of Shishu-Sji in Zirmazd's tower.

'Gods!' snapped a familiar voice, contemptuously.

'Torr!' cried Tara, and he felt warm arms about him.

He opened his eyes wearily, yet buoyed up by the victory won.

All his muscles trembled like young stallions from the fierceness of the conflict. He shuddered, and breathed deep, and gave thanks that he was still alive.

'Oh, Torr – it was dreadful!'

'Aye, for one who believes what they see!'

Tara flashed at the Pragmatist. 'I saw a great smoke and a shining conflict, gruesome forms and the flash of weapons! I know what I saw, here in the skull chamber –'

'The Black Bodice . . .' said Torr Vorkun, with difficulty.

Tara sat him in Zirmazd's great chair whilst that shrunken wizard wrung his hands, and bathed him and soothed him. Torr looked across to where the astral projection of Shishu-Sji smiled at him from beside the empty golden cage where Ishrivara of the golden feathers had spent her long imprisonment.

'Lunga-Tuchulchya,' he said, hoarsely, 'the familiar from the pit you knew as Sjik! Summon him! Call him and then use the tooth of Black Nargoth on him! Destroy him utterly!'

'That pleasure, Kar Torr, has already been vouchsafed me. Look!' Shushi-Sji flung up a ghostly arm.

Within the black and scarlet pentacle a toad-thing scurried, seeking escape, and finding none. Its grotesque legs shrivelled, its scaly hide smoked and sloughed. Last to disappear into a tiny blob of green slime were its hollow orbs that smoked until the end.

Zirmazd the Wily moaned.

In a great flutter of wings and the clashing of bronze accoutrements the teryxes brought their outriders down on the castle of Gamelon Town, forerunners of the investing host. Kar Sjontu strode into the chamber with a wrinkle of his nose and a: 'By Dalku-Darn, the place smells of the sjeed lines unattended for a fortnight!'

Standing up, still clutching Lycheaper, Torr gave the knight welcome.

'Now may your people take possession of this place, Kar Sjontu,' he said gravely. 'I know nothing of the rights and wrongs of a whole people thus migrating and taking over another habitation. But I do know what my sister and I – and Frelgar – suffered here. You are very welcome.'

'You'll stay, Kar Torr! There will be a high place for you with us, with the Sjomban line. And I know, assuredly, that the lady Meline of Sjomba will smile kindly upon you –'

'Nay, nay, friend Sjontu. That cannot be. For I must seek out Jaran the All-seeing. It is a bond – a loving bond of duty and affection, laid on me.'

The ghostly form of the Sjombalkuan wizard vanished and moments later his flesh and blood body slid nimbly from a teryx and entered the skull chamber, smiling like a man on his bridal night.

'Good Torr Vorkun! Right well you carried out your compact. And now, I will honour my own pledge. When you are rested I will tell you all I know of Jaran the All-seeing. You will be fully equiped and outfitted – we will speed you on your way with laughter and with song, and also with sorrow that you depart from us.'

'Thank you, Shishu-Sji. All the western world awaits our search.'

'We will find him,' said Tara Vorkun, confidently. 'For the sake of our dear foster-father, Vorkun the Wise, we will find him!'

'Gods and sorcerers!' sniffed Frelgar the Pragmatist. 'Oh, well, for the sake of man's humanity to man, I think I'd best accompany these two twins. How they've managed to survive so long without me to guide them I really can't imagine!'

'Pragmatist!' scoffed Torr Vorkun of Darkholm of Drugay, with the deep knowledge of one who has battled the gods and won.

And Tara Vorkun of Darkholm looked up at her twin brother, and squeezed his arm in sisterly affection.